GEM OF UNCERTAINTY

CAMILLE MICHAELS

This is a work of fiction. Names, characters, businesses, places, events, and incidents are either the products of the author's imagination or used in a fictitious manner. Any resemblance to actual persons, living or dead, or actual events is purely coincidental.

ISBN: 978-1-7356416-2-1

DEDICATION

To my sister, my lifelong companion, who was cut from the same cloth and can always laugh at and sympathize with many of my thoughts and feelings in this sometimes strange and unnerving world.

CHAPTER ONE

Gemma! For the love of God, don't do this. Don't. Don't you dare.

My eyelids slowly roll open.

You did it. Why'd you do it?

It's Saturday at 7:57 A.M.

Close them. Close them back up right this second.

I roll onto my back, lift my right hand, run my fingers through my hair, and then raise both arms into a stretch.

Gemma, I swear. This is not the time to get up.

I have to get ready. I am meeting Nate for tea at ten.

That's not for a couple of hours, and why did you just call him Nate?

That's his name.

Nope. Don't like it. He's McGruff.

So, I should just call him McGruff for the rest of his life?

Yes.

Fine for now. I have to get ready to see McGruff.

Fine, since you are clearly not going back to sleep now.

I roll out of bed, shower, blow dry my hair, get dressed, and sit at the counter in the kitchen portion of my studio apartment. I stare at my single serve coffee maker.

"Hello, old friend." I sigh. "One day we will be back together."

When I stopped drinking coffee and caffeine all together, I didn't think that I would survive a week, never mind three months. My anxiety had gotten so bad, I started to see a therapist, and she suggested that I give up caffeine completely. I do love my coffee, but I hate my anxiety even more. Giving it up was not easy to do, and, to the surprise of no one at all, neither is coping with and treating anxiety. I started medication about two months ago, and even that does not seem to help.

Anxiety is a disease without a cure. Therapy and medication are most definitely not a cure. They are walking sticks. I must go up the mountain myself. And I must say, it is a hard climb.

No, don't think like that. You just have to give it time.

I have given it time! And I am still anxious.

Just breathe. McGruff will make you feel better.

I don't even want to go to meet McGruff.

Why? It's a beautiful day, you get to see charming McGruff. You will get out of your apartment, and you will get some sunlight in your life.

I just don't feel like leaving my apartment.

Gemma. You are already out of bed and dressed. You have to go. McGruff is waiting for you. You want to see McGruff, don't you?

Yeah. I guess.

You guess? Of course, you want to see him. You already canceled on him last night because you said you were too tired.

I was too tired.

And you got a full three hours of sleep last night. That's more than you usually get. You need to make an effort here.

I don't want to.

Yes, you do. Gemma, I swear, if you don't go…

If I don't go, what?

He will stop forgiving you your nonsense.

My nonsense?

You know what I mean.

No, I don't. If he doesn't like me like this, then he doesn't like me at all.

That is not true, Gemma.

He should be able to handle me when I am like anything. He should. And I am not sure…

You aren't sure, what? That he does?

Whoever I am with should be able to accept me as is. What, no come back for that one?

2

No. Whoever you are with should be able to accept you as you are.

And is that McGruff?

I guess you will just have to find out. And you won't be able to find out if you never leave your apartment and never see him.

I guess that is true.

It is true. So, get out the door, and go meet McGruff.

Fine.

And try to be a little more positive, please? Can you do that?

I am not sure.

Yes, you can!

It's summertime in Boston, which means that the heat and humidity are chipping slowly away at my, now minimal, motivation to leave my apartment. Lucky, the humidity has not rolled in yet this morning, but it is expected this afternoon. It is the beginning of another heat wave, so it will be ninety degrees or above for at least three days in a row. As I open the door to exit my apartment building, the heat hits me in the face.

Yuck. As if I haven't been sweating enough. It's like I'm a sweat factory lately. Even sitting in front of the air conditioner doesn't help. I am constantly dripping. Thank goodness my apartment building is air-conditioned. I don't know what I would do if it weren't.

Why did I agree to walk to the Common on such a gross day? I am not going to make it back in the humidity. I should just go back.

No. You canceled on McGruff once this weekend already. You're not canceling last minute. He's probably already waiting for you at Sally's.

And that, he is. As I ding through the door, he turns with an iced coffee in one hand and an iced tea in the other. His usually hypnotizing, blue eyes look at me.

"I hope this is okay," he says. "She doesn't have decaf tea."

"I know."

Gem of Uncertainty

What the hell, Gemma? That's all you are going to say? That's super bitchy. Look at Sally's face. She looks upset with you. At least, say thank you.

"Thanks."

Sally's is a small coffee shop near my apartment building. I come here every day, or I used to when I drank coffee. Sally and I are friends, which was inevitable since I am here in the morning and occasionally in afternoon for dinner. At the moment, McGruff and I are the only two in the shop. It is relatively small, with a few tables and a countertop with a showcase below it that has baked goods in the morning and a casserole or macaroni and cheese in the afternoon and evening.

McGruff hands me the tea and asks, "Are you okay?" Raising a hand, he flicks his hand through his short, light-brown hair and then nervously strokes his beard. Both his hair and beard have tiny white flecks just starting to show.

No. I wish I hadn't agreed to this stupid walk. It's stupid hot outside, and it's only going to get hotter.

"I'm fine." I fake a smile.

McGruff fakes his own smile.

I met McGruff about three months ago. Actually, I didn't really meet him until a few weeks later. Maybe I should say McGruff started to come into my orbit three months ago. I would see him around Norman B. Leventhal Park, the park near the office where I sometimes go for lunch, and I would see him in the elevator or lobby of the building. He works two floors down and was always so stern, I never knew if he liked me or if he felt obligated to talk to me for some reason, which is why I dubbed him McGruff. Obviously, he doesn't know about the nickname. He then started showing up at Flannery's, the bar I go to on Saturdays with my best friend. Eventually, when I no longer had full blown panic attacks around him, he asked me out, and we started dating. It's been over a month since then, and things have been going well. Rather, things were going well up until recently.

You used to think he was gruff. Look at you now. You are the gruff one. Maybe he has internally nicknamed you McGruff.

That would actually be sort of awesome.

"You two have fun now," Sally says as McGruff leads me out the door. I can see her eyes narrow as she shakes her head of brown hair and pushes the grey hairs around the temple behind her ear.

Oh, I won't. There is no way I am having fun.

Geez, Gemma. Try, would you?

Okay, there is a slight chance I will have fun.

You are looking pretty McGruffy to me.

Fine. I will try to have fun.

McGruff and I start towards the Boston Common, which is about a ten-minute walk from my apartment building. I go there a lot to clear my mind, a feat that is not actually possible. My mind is never clear.

"How are you today?" McGruff asks.

"Hot and sweaty."

"Are you feeling any better than you did last night?"

"Not really."

Gemma, I swear, be nice. What are you doing? He hasn't done anything to make you upset. You just said you would try to be nice.

"Okay. I didn't want to do this, but you've left me no choice."

He stops, grabs my waist, and proceeds to tickle me.

"No!" I yell and struggle away from him. "I don't know why people think tickling will put people into a good mood."

"You're laughing, aren't you?"

"It's forced laughter. There is nothing fun about being tickled."

"Then why are you still smiling?"

"Shut up."

I really am in a better mood. This so isn't fair. I deserve to be in a crappy mood if I want to be. It's not right that there is an override button on crappy moods.

Why would you *want* to be in a crappy mood?

It's just the principle of the matter. I shouldn't be forced into being happy if I don't want to be.

Do you even hear yourself right now?

"Do you want to sit for a little while?" McGruff slows down, turns slightly towards me, and looks hesitantly into my eyes.

I hadn't even noticed, but we have arrived at the Boston Common. There are people everywhere, and I can feel the temperature rising by the second.

No. Let's go straight home. Beat the humidity.

Gemma, sit.

"Sure," I say.

"Good. Let's go sit by the Swan Boats."

"Okay."

The Swan Boats are mostly a tourist attraction in the Boston Public Garden, next to the Common. They are boats with benches and giant swans on the back in which the driver of the boat sits.

We sit down on a bench in front of the people getting on and off the boats. McGruff puts his arm around my shoulder, leans over, and kisses me on the forehead. I instinctively put my head on his shoulder.

There. You feel better now, don't you?

I must admit. I do.

See. He's good for you.

"I'm sorry I've been so cranky. The heat and humidity really get to me," I say.

He rests his cheek on my head.

"Don't worry about it. The heat gets to everyone."

I look around at the people on the Swan Boats and over to the people throwing frisbees, kicking around soccer balls, and walking down the paths holding hands, and I remember when I would come here alone with a book and be envious of all these people. Now, here I am with McGruff sipping iced tea. And I am still not happy.

But, I do feel more content than I did back then, my crankiness notwithstanding. Even with that, McGruff seems to ease just by being here.

Aren't you glad that you came? You are less anxious than you were before you left your apartment this morning.

Yeah, I suppose. I still don't feel right. I don't feel like myself.

McGruff runs his hand over my hair and kisses me on the top of the head. My eyes close as I breathe in.

"Are you going out with Liz, tonight?" he asks.

"Yeah. I think if I cancel on her, she will kill me."

"Good."

"Good? You want her to kill me?"

"Maybe a little earlier."

"Hey!" I sit up and punch him in the arm.

"You know I would never kill you," he says as he places his palm on my cheek. "We've established I'm not an axe murderer, remember?"

"Why do you have to bring that up all time?"

"Because it's adorable."

"We never did establish that you weren't a stalker."

"No. But you did agree to go out with me, so I think the situation worked out."

"Speak for yourself."

"Hey!" He gently punches me on the arm.

"What?" I laugh. "You definitely stalked me for a little while."

"It was the only way I could get you to talk to me. And I actually really like Flannery's. I mean, I would have gone there even if you weren't there. That place is cool."

"Hands off my place."

"I know. I know. Besides, my own bar, O'Brady's would be jealous if I left."

"I bet."

"You are so beautiful when you smile."

"You're a dork."

Oh, my God, Gemma. Will you please learn how to respond to a compliment? That is not even close to what you should have said.

"I know. I'm a giant dork."

A goofy smile spreads across his face. I smile, myself, as I watch his eyes light up.

I swipe a line of sweat that is literally dripping down my forehead. Glancing at McGruff, he looks cool as a cucumber. How is that even possible? How come I get the genes that make me a sweat monster, and he gets to remain as beautiful as ever, even when the humidity is creeping up?

"Are you okay?" he asks.

"No. I am a giant hot mess."

He sighs. "You want to go home, then?"

No. Say no.

"Yes."

Gemma, you should stay.

No. It's gross out. I will melt into a puddle if I stay out here long enough. That's attractive, isn't it?

My phone buzzes, and I pull it out of my purse to check the text message. It's Liz. Her message says, "Don't you dare cancel on me again! I want to see you tonight!"

Great. I sigh.

"Something wrong?" McGruff asks.

"No, it's just Liz. She is making sure I am going out with her tonight."

"Are you?"

"I guess I have to."

"Are you okay?"

"Yeah. I am fine. Why are you always asking me that?"

"Because you don't seem like you are. You've been canceling on Liz. You've been canceling on me. I am just worried."

"I'm fine. I've just been really tired."

8

"For weeks?"

"Yes! For weeks!"

"Okay."

I see him recoil and cross his arms over his chest.

Damn it, Gemma. Why are you being such a jerk?

My phone buzzes again. This time it is my coworker Nick. He is letting me know that P2 has successfully been implemented. It is the second phase of the three-phase project that has been years in the making. Nick had to work today to move the code into production, poor guy.

"Liz again?" McGruff asks.

"No, it's Nick. He's just letting me know that the P2 go-live is over, and everything went fine."

"That's nice of him."

"Yeah, it is."

Putting my phone back in my purse, I can feel McGruff staring at me. I turn to look at him.

"Don't you dare ask me if I'm okay."

"I wouldn't dare. Shall we go?"

"Yes."

Gemma, you are a cranky tooth tiger. Why are you being so mean to him? You are being a McGruff Allstar. He is just concerned.

There is no reason to be concerned.

Isn't there?

Gemma, you completely ruined a perfectly good day. What is going on with you?

I honestly don't know.

We barely speak on the walk back, only agreeing to part ways in front of my apartment building. He slowly walks away, still holding my hand, until he is too far. His wide eyes search mine.

My eyes soften for a moment, and my lips turn into a smile.

"Bye," I say.

He smiles. "Bye, warrior princess."

I roll my eyes and turn to walk into my building.

Won't he ever stop calling me that?

Probably not. The first time you went out with him, you did call yourself a warrior princess, claiming that you don't need saving, as you are not a damsel in distress.

Well, I'm not!

Yeah, got it. Just try to not be so beastly to Liz, later. Okay?

No promises.

Gemma, seriously.

I can't control it. I don't know what is happening to me. Maybe I just don't really like McGruff.

That's not true. Did you not just see yourself smile coyly at him as he left? And that would mean that you don't like Liz either then because you have had the same attitude with her. You keep canceling on her as well.

No, Liz is my best friend. I don't know why I am acting like this.

Try to be nice to her. To everyone, actually.

Fine. Just let me lie down for a little while. I didn't get any sleep last night.

Back in my apartment, I lie down on my bed and set my alarm, just in case. But I know that I won't actually sleep. Sleep is just a myth to me. It is just beyond my grasp. It is uncatchable, and my anxiety is inescapable.

Apparently, so is your bitchiness.

Touché.

Pulling open the door to Flannery's, I feel the cool air from inside and am suddenly almost glad that Liz made me go out tonight. Inside, the air-conditioned pub is a welcome relief from the heat and humidity outside.

The pub is relatively small, only about twelve tables litter the floor, with a jukebox and a pool table in the corner. The mahogany bar lines the wall overlooking the seating area with a mirror behind it, but that is mostly blocked by the televisions and the assortment of alcohol bottles.

Liz is already seated at the bar and in conversation with the bartender Greg, who is leaning on the bar in front of her. They both turn to look at me as if they had just finished talking about me.

"Hey guys," I say and pull out a chair next to Liz and sit down.

Liz fluffs her golden hair, looks at me with her brown eyes, and raises an eyebrow at me. We have been best friends since we met at Boston University. I came with her to Flannery's all the time when she tried to get Brett, her now husband, to ask her out.

"Hey there, beautiful," Greg says. "I am glad Liz forced you to come out tonight. I haven't seen you for a couple of weeks." Greg stands up straight and puts his hands on his hips. He has baby blue eyes, a chiseled jaw, and a blonde man-bun.

"She did not force me to come out," I respond.

"That's not what I hear," Greg says, shrugs his shoulders, and walks away to pour my drink.

"I did force you," Liz says and turns her body to face me. "You canceled on me two Saturdays in a row."

"I'm sorry. I haven't been feeling up to anything."

"I had to hang out with Brett," she says and smiles.

"I know. It is such a horrible fate to hang out with your own, good looking, funny husband. Must have been horrible for you."

"It was! I missed you!"

"I missed you, too," Greg says as he places my drink down in front of me. "What have you been doing with yourself? Seeing that guy of yours?"

I shake my head. "I've just been staying in mostly."

"Hmm," Greg says, raising an eyebrow before walking away to help someone else.

I turn to look out over the pub. This is a bar where everyone knows everyone else, and people give no thought to talking to whoever is at their side, even if they know them or not. Usually, that comradery is a welcome event.

"What's wrong?" Liz asks.

"I was hoping for a table."

"Why?"

"I don't feel like talking to anyone."

"Even me?"

"Besides you."

"Okay. Do you want to move over there in the corner?"

"Yes."

I push my chair out and grab my drink. Liz does the same. We walk over to the table in the corner of the pub with no one around, and we sit. I can see Greg, with arms crossed, staring at us from behind the bar.

"So?" Liz says.

"So? There is nothing to talk about. I just don't feel like talking to anyone."

"Why?"

"I don't know! I just don't. And I am tired."

"Why didn't you stay home tonight?"

"Because you made me go out, remember?"

"I didn't mean to make you go out. I'm sorry if I made you feel like I forced you to."

"It's fine. I am here now."

Liz sips quietly on her drink for a few moments.

Damn it, Gemma. Why did you have to be so mean? She only wants to see her best friend, and you are being a giant bitch. You said you would try to be nice.

I don't know. I can't even stop it. I should tell people to call me McGruff now.

"Did you go out with Nate last night?" Liz asks.

"No. I saw him this morning."

"What did you do last night then?"

"Nothing."

"Nothing?"

"Yeah, nothing."

"Why'd you cancel on Nate?"

"I didn't feel like going out."

"What did Stacey say?"

"I didn't go to see her either."

"You canceled on Stacey, too?"

"Yeah. I didn't feel like talking to my therapist about...anything."

"Gemma, what is going on? You've canceled on me the last couple of weeks. I practically had to beg you to come out today."

"I'm tired all the time, yet I can't sleep." I wipe the sweat from my forehead. "And I sweat constantly."

"What does your medication provider say? What is her name again, Janet?"

"Yeah. She upped my dose two weeks ago. I go back in two more weeks."

"How long does it take to work?"

"It could take up to twelve weeks."

"Twelve weeks!"

"Yep."

"How was Nate this morning? What did you do?"

"We just walked to the Common, and then I went home to try to nap, but I couldn't, so I sat in front of the air conditioner in my apartment because I could feel myself melting."

"How are you two doing?"

"Bad."

"Bad?"

"Yeah. I am constantly snapping at him, and I don't know why. I'm not me anymore. I can't control it."

"You have to try to cut him some slack."

"I know, Liz! Don't you think I know that?"

That was bitchy. Bitchy McBitch Face.

"I'm sorry, Liz. You should have let me cancel tonight. I'm not myself. I didn't mean to yell at you."

Liz reaches across the table and grabs my forearm.

"It's okay, Gemma."

"I'm still sorry."

"I know."

"I don't deserve you."

"I know that, too."

CHAPTER TWO

It is another hot and humid day. Not even eight in the morning yet, and it already feels like I am walking through a sauna. I can almost feel my hair frizzing out. As I walk down to my office building in a skirt, short sleeved blouse, and heals, sweat is dripping down my forehead.

Yuck. I will probably be soaked by the time I get to my desk.

It's only a few more minutes, and you'll be in the air conditioning all day.

My office building is just a few blocks away from my apartment building. I live in a studio because I can't afford anything bigger in this part of the city, which is called Downtown Crossing. It has stores and restaurants within walking distance of my apartment, so I like living here. The area that my office is in, also within walking distance, is called the Financial District.

I work at an insurance company as a business analyst. I do like my job, if only I weren't required to go to so many meetings. They are, or rather feel, like actual torture. Anyone who has never experienced anxiety would not understand that statement and may ask why I still have this job if it tortures me every day. My answer is that I want to be normal. I try so hard to be normal like everyone else. I fight daily to do the things that come so naturally to other people, *so* naturally, that they don't even think about them. I, on the other hand, obsess about and dread them.

Looking down, I slightly raise my arm and check my armpit for sweat stains.

Don't worry. You're here.

Opening the door to the building, the cool air washes over my body. I run my hands over my now frizzy hair and inconspicuously air out my armpits.

Gem of Uncertainty

I have to wait only a few minutes before the elevator opens, and I step over the slit of death, which is what I call the hole between the elevator floor and the building floor. The heel of my shoe once got stuck in there, and it is something I now perpetually avoid. I step over the slit of death and into the box with six other sweaty messes. One by one, they leave. The last woman gets out on the eighteenth floor. As she walks past the banner that reads, "Today is the Day!" I roll my eyes.

Today is never the day. At least, not when I am here.

Those poor people on that floor. Do they even look at that banner anymore? Do they hate it as much as I do? Do they hate it more than I do? Can they secretly tear it down for the good of the building?

The traveling box stops on the twenty-second floor, and I once again step over the slit of death, only to be nearly hip checked into the wall by Barb, who is speed walking down the hall.

"Watch where you're going!" she snaps and brushes back her brown hair.

Good morning to you, too, Bitch Queen.

Barbara is still a pain in my ass and is constantly judging everything I do when she is not roller derby checking me into walls. Despite being in her fifties, she still acts like she is in high school. She is one of the project managers here, just like my boss Carl.

If only she would retire soon. No, if only Jack would retire soon.

You aren't lucky enough for that. Your nemesis will never retire. He will outlive us all.

No, but I've been lucky the past two months not to have to be in the daily morning meeting with him. I've had very little contact with him recently.

Don't. You just jinxed it. I swear, if you just jinxed it...

But it's been so nice. My days aren't nearly as stressful as they used to be.

Oh, my God. Knock on wood, would you? You are going to ruin this amazing reprieve.

Nick is already at his desk when I walk by. His dark brown hair is as disheveled as ever, though his beard is trimmed this morning. He is a web programmer and is, or was, my best work friend before Brittany started working here in the underwriting department. Out of the corner of my eye, I can see his head pop up as I walk by. I sit down in my cubicle directly next to his, with a partition between us, high enough so that we can't see each other. Joe comes in a few minutes later and sits on the other side of and across the aisle from me. He is also a business analyst, which is unfortunate, because he is actually really nice, but because we both do the same job, we rarely work on the same projects. The rest of the cubes fill up in minutes.

Oh, the joy of the beginning of a brand new day. What fresh hell awaits me today? Only time will tell. I am sure it will be something. It always is.

At least, you don't have to go to the daily morning meeting where Jack yells everyday, Bill argues, and Nick and Ed snicker together in the back of the room.

At least, there's that miracle. I do feel a little bad that I left Brittany in there all alone. But not enough to go back without being physically forced.

I smirk at Nick as he walks by, his dark brown eyes glaring at me. It's time for the daily meeting, and Carl has yet to mention when he is making me go back.

Don't jinx it. I swear, you just jinxed it.

My company is in the middle of a project to move all of our policyholders from our old legacy computer system to a new, web-based, administration system. It will take years, and we are now in Phase 3, or P3, the final phase of the project now that P2 went live over the weekend. The part of the company-wide project that I am a part of, we have nicknamed Bookroll because we are rolling our book of business to our new computer system. It is still, by far, the most hated part of the project. Lucky me.

Gem of Uncertainty

I watch as Carl, Bill, Jack, and Ed walk down towards the conference room and hear a click when the door shuts. Carl, my boss, is the project manager. Bill is QA, or quality assurance, and does the testing. Jack is the mainframe COBOL programmer, and Ed is the data warehouse expert. The project moves our entire book of business, or policies, from the old mainframe to the new, web-based, administration portal. We are, in fact, making Jack's job obsolete.

Oh, please let that be true. Oh, please let that be true.

The daily meeting is the first meeting in the morning and is a recap of the prior day, defects, responsibilities, and expectations. I do not envy them in there. But then again P2 went live this past weekend, so it won't be long before Carl makes me go back. I really did enjoy my time off though. I just wish it could last forever.

As I open a new email, there is a low hum and then silence.

"Not again." I hear someone say from across the room. It is more of an exasperated sigh.

The white noise has gone out again. There is usually a constant hum of white noise all over the building, presumably to keep sounds from echoing across the department. It is usually imperceptible, for I have grown accustomed to hearing it throughout the day. And now that it is gone, I can hear literally everyone typing on their keyboards all over the department.

I cannot work like this.

It's fine. Just ignore everyone.

But everyone can hear everything I do. Every time I move in my chair, I feel like the whole company can hear the chair squeak.

Well, they probably can.

That's helpful.

Just being honest, Ms. McGruff.

That name is not going to be a thing.

I sigh. Well, there goes my motivation to work.

The key to not doing any work at work is to look busy. I need to look busy physically. I can be just moving the mouse back and forth and my eyes can be unfocussed, but as long as it looks like I am working, then I am golden. If my eyes are in the direction of my monitor, and my hand moves the mouse every once in a while, to everyone else, I look like I am working. If I furrow my brow to look like I am deep in thought, even better.

I am doing just that as Nick and Brittany appear before me as they are leaving the daily meeting. I look up.

"You look really busy," Brittany says to me.

Ha! Yes, I do.

"I can spare a minute for you two. How was the meeting?"

"It was fine," Nick says. "It was basically just a debrief of the go-live this weekend. Everything went fine. Nothing out of the ordinary happened."

"When are you coming back to us?" Brittany asks me.

"Hopefully never. But I know Carl will make me eventually. Probably soon. I can feel it."

"Well, we miss you in there," Brittany says.

Brittany stops talking as Bob, our vice president, walks behind them. She and Nick both roll their eyes and scatter. The walk-by is the universal indicator that it's time to go back to your own desk.

I can hear Nick through the partition next to me as he sits in his chair, types on his keyboard, and clicks his mouse a few times.

"Is it really quiet in here?" he asks.

I'm not sure if he's directing that question to me, but I respond with, "Yes, the white noise is out again."

"Damn it!" Nick yells.

"Whoa there, killer," Joe says from his cube on the other side of mine, across the aisle. "No need to yell so that the whole company can hear you. I have sensitive ears over here," he jokes.

"So sorry," Nick speaks at his normal volume, which now is plenty loud enough for Joe to hear. "I will refrain from yelling for the near future."

"Much appreciated," Joe responds.

Smiling, I look over at Joe, who smirks at me.

"Oh, the HVAC unit is being fixed again," I hear Nick say as I open my most recent email and read the same.

"That thing is a piece of crap," Ed says from the row over. He sits behind Nick.

"If it gets to be over eighty degrees in here, I am out," Larry says from the other side of Nick.

"If it gets to be seventy degrees, *I* am out," Fred adds from behind me.

"Please, if this white noise is off any longer, I am out," Andy pipes up from the back of the row next to mine.

"This conversation brought to you by the broken HVAC unit," George says from the row over.

Everyone in my row and the row next to mine laughs, including me. We all can't usually talk to each other like this unless the white noise is off. I guess there is one good thing about it going out.

Oh, my God, Gemma. Did you just say that being able to talk to your coworkers is a good thing?

What? I guess, I did. Something must be wrong with me.

Well, obviously.

I pull up my calendar. Only two meetings today. That's not so bad. My monthly one-on-one meeting with Carl and the monthly department meeting, also run by Carl. Could be worse.

"Gemma?"

What the heck? Is that Ed talking to me from the row over?

"Yes?" I say at a normal voice level.

"I am finishing up the changes to the requirements. I will send them over in a few minutes."

"Okay, thanks, Ed."

"Oh!" Nick shouts. "I have to send you mine, too."

"Copycat," Ed teases.

"What did I say about shouting?" Joe asks.

"Oh! Sorry, Joe!" Nick responds.

20

Within a few minutes, I have received both emails from Nick and Ed and have already started updating my requirements spreadsheet.

So much for only pretending to work today.

It's better that I have work to do. If no one heard me type, then they'd know I wasn't working. I can hear everyone else typing.

Just then the white noise comes back on.

"Oh, thank God!" I hear someone yell from across the department.

Someone is happy. It must be the same person I heard earlier when the noise went off.

I spend the next two hours updating requirements, and before I know it, Carl is walking past my desk to get to our monthly meeting.

What the? He is early. I am usually the one who is early. What is happening today?

I gather my pen and pad of paper, follow him into the conference room, and close the door behind me. Carl is an African-American man in his early sixties. He sometimes acts more like a father than he does my boss, but lately it has been all boss.

"How is everything?" he asks as we sit across from each other at the table.

Shitty, McShit Shit. Thank you for asking.

"Everything is fine."

"Good. You heard that P2 went live this weekend?"

"Yes. That is good news."

"Yes, it is very exciting. Are you going to the party on Friday?"

Shit. Can I say no? Is that appropriate? Can I say yes and then not go? Is that more appropriate?

How about you say that you are going and then actually go?

That is not an option.

"I think I am, yes," I respond.

"Good. It should be fun. We all spent a lot of time getting this project implemented. We deserve a celebration. It's a nice thing that Bob is doing for us."

Yeah. You have to go.

That is TBD.

"What have you been working on lately?" he asks.

"I am almost done with the warehouse requirements and the rollout schedule for P3."

"How are the web and mainframe requirements coming along?"

"I am still working through them."

"I want you to set up recurring meetings with both Nick and Jack, separately, at least twice a week until you have the requirements finished. We need to hit the ground running with P3."

I think I just had a stroke. He wants me to meet with Jack by myself? At least twice a week?

"That's not how we did it for P2."

"Well, that's how we are doing it for P3. Can you do that?"

No! Tell him no. Tell him there is no way in hell you are doing that.

"Yes."

"Okay, good. I also wanted to talk to you about being more outgoing in meetings. You barely speak at all. I know you have a lot of knowledge, and I'd like you to share it."

Be more outgoing. Of course, so simple. Why didn't I think of that? It's like every teacher and boss I've ever had hasn't said that exact same thing to me. Mrs. Branch, my English teacher in eleventh grade, failing me for not talking enough. Mr. Costell, my middle school guidance counselor, telling me I am not good enough because I don't speak in class. Mrs. Patters in elementary school, telling me that I will never make it in life if I don't learn to speak up.

Why didn't I think just to be more outgoing? It's so easy to do, right? Everyone else seems to think so.

"Can you do that?" Carl asks.

Can I do that? No, I can't do that. I have never done that, and I will never do that. It is not possible. This is me. I cannot change this. No, I cannot do that.

"Sure."

What the hell, Gemma? Tell him that you can't. Tell him that it isn't fair to hold you to these requirements set for everyone else. Tell him.

Tell him what? That everyone in my life has told me the exact same thing? Why should I think he'd be any different? He has already shown me that he is not. He will not understand.

It's okay, Gemma. Just swim a little. Keep your head above the water just enough to get out of this meeting. It is fine. It is not worth getting upset over this stupid mandate from Carl. You have been through this before, and you will go through this again. You will be fine. You always are. People just don't understand.

"Okay. Good. And we need to get you back into the daily morning meeting. I will let you know when to return."

No! You didn't knock on wood, did you? You jinxed it!

"Okay," I murmur.

"Anything else you'd like to talk about?" Carl asks.

"No."

"All right. Set up those meetings. And I am sure I will talk to you soon. If you need anything in the meantime, let me know."

"Great. Thank you."

Carl gets up and walks out of the room. I slowly get up out of my chair and walk down the aisle back to my desk. Brittany is standing in front of Nick's desk talking to Nick as I sit down.

"Do you want to go to lunch at the park with me and Nick?" she asks me.

"Yuck," I respond.

"Did you just yuck us? You heard that right, Nick?"

"Oh, I heard it."

"I didn't yuck *you*. I yucked the weather. It's so hot."

"So, what? You're just going to eat alone at your desk?" Brittany asks.

"Yeah."

"Yuck," Brittany responds.

"Don't you yuck me."

"You yucked me!" Brittany replies.

"It's so gross out," I say.

"We will sit in the shade," Brittany retorts.

"We will sit on the side of the fountain, and we will splash you periodically," Nick says through the wall.

"It's the perfect plan," Brittany says.

"I'm going to regret this," I murmur.

"Yes!" Brittany shouts. "No, not that you are going to regret it because you won't."

"You might a little," Nick adds.

"And speaking of things you are going to go to, you are going to the P2 party on Friday, right?" she asks me.

Not this again. I can say no to Brittany and not feel bad when I don't go.

Can you?

"You need to go," she says. "Nick, tell her that she needs to go to the party on Friday night."

"Gemma, you need to go," Nick says through the wall.

"See." She smiles at me.

"Aren't you guys chummy, now?"

"Friendship forged in the fires of the daily meeting. You know how that is."

"I'd like to forget."

"You survived the daily meetings all year. You need to go to the go-live celebration. You already accepted it, anyway. You told me you did."

"I wish I hadn't."

"Oh, come on! Free drinks, free food, it will be fun."

"Fun? Have you ever been to a work party before?"

"Well, actually, no. This will be my first. And it's my first at this company, too. And I want you to be there."

24

You should go, Gemma.

But...

No, buts. You should go.

"Is your silence a yes?" Brittany asks.

It's definitely not a yes.

"You've never been to a work party?" I ask.

"No. So you need to come. Please? They aren't allowing plus ones. You need to be there to hang out with me."

"And me!" Nick shouts through the wall.

Brittany smiles again. "You know you want to."

"Oh, I definitely don't want to."

"But?"

"But...I will."

"Yes!" Brittany claps twice and grins. She then turns, leans over to Nick's desk, and says, "We got her!"

"Yes!"

Brittany leans back. "We got you," she says, looks me directly in the eyes, and walks away.

Why did you just agree to that?

I already accepted it. And I dealt with the daily meetings all year. I should celebrate.

You just don't want to see McGruff.

What? That has nothing to do with it.

So, you admit that you don't want to see him?

Shut up!

Brittany returns at lunchtime and stands in front of my desk and stares at me until I lock my computer and go with them.

You should never have said yes. You are going to regret going. You are going to melt into a puddle out there.

And I do. The second the door to the building opens, it's like I've walked into a brick wall. The humidity is close to a hundred percent, and I have trouble breathing. Sweat does not waste any time, and immediately begins to roll down my forehead.

"Yuck," I say.

"It's not that bad," Brittany replies.

I grimace and glare at her.

"It's pretty bad," Nick responds.

"Thank you!" I say.

Lagging behind them on the way to the park, I try to mop my forehead and air out my armpits. We all get lunch at the café, and as they promised, we find a table in the shade. I sit and close my eyes to compose myself.

"Are you okay?" Nick asks me.

"Yeah, I just need to not move a muscle the whole time I am out here."

"Yeah, it's pretty gross," he says.

"It's not that bad," Brittany repeats. She turns to me as I use my napkin to wipe off my entire face.

"That's garbage," Nick says.

"Garbage?" Brittany asks.

"Yeah. Whenever I code something wrong, if I miss a semicolon or something, it says, 'There's garbage after your expression.'"

"Jeepers," Brittany responds.

"Yeah, it's pretty harsh."

"Well, it's a computer. It doesn't know it's hurting your feelings," Brittany says.

"Well, a human programmed it to say that. Unless, it was Skynet," Nick replies.

I laugh.

"Skynet?" Brittany asks.

"Not a Terminator fan?" Nick asks her.

"I don't even know what that means," she responds.

"Oh, my God. I can't believe I agreed to go to lunch with you," Nick says.

Brittany laughs and turns to look at me as I scan the entire park. I can't bear to move my head in this humidity. Why did I agree to go out at lunch?

"Who are you looking for?" Brittany asks me.

"No one."

"Are you worried Nate is going to find you here lunch cheating on him?"

"Well, he does have a habit of showing up where I am."

"That's a good point."

"Who is Nate?" Nick asks.

"Gemma's guy," Brittany responds.

"Gemma has a guy?"

He seems shocked. Does he not think I can get a guy?

I mean, probably not. You are a hot mess.

"Yep," Brittany says. "He works a couple of floors down at Digitize Tech."

Nick looks at me, and I awkwardly smile.

"You've been seeing McGruff for a couple months now?" Brittany asks.

"McGruff?" Nick asks. "Who is McGruff?"

Oh my God. Why did she have to say that?

Brittany looks shyly at me. "Sorry," she says.

"McGruff?" Nick asks again.

"That may be what I call him," I answer.

He laughs. "Is it serious?"

McGruff and I? Are we serious?

Gemma, they are waiting for you to answer. Brittany can't answer this one.

Are you sure? She can definitely answer just about anything.

Yes, this is a question you need to answer.

"I'm not sure I'd call it serious. It's only been a couple of months."

"Oh." He seems...relieved?

27

"He seems pretty serious about you," Brittany says.

See! She could have answered!

"Yeah. He'll get over that," I respond.

"Gemma!" Brittany scolds.

"Brittany."

She rolls her eyes. "Okay. Let's talk about the party at Fenway, then."

"Ugh."

Brittany side eyes me. "You're going," she says flatly.

"Well, I'm excited," Nick says.

"So am I!" Brittany replies.

They both look at me.

Oh, is it my turn to say that I am excited? Because I am not. I've already told Carl and these two that I am going, isn't that enough? Do I have to pretend to be happy about it now?

Geez, Ms. McGruff.

I shrug.

"How was your meeting with Carl?" Nick asks me.

"Oh, my God. He wants me to set up one-on-one meetings with both you and Jack. I don't think I can handle that."

"Oh, come on Nick isn't that bad," Brittany jokes.

"I am, actually," he responds. "But seriously, with Jack? That is a fate worse than death."

"Tell me about it. I am going to set up my meeting with Jack right before yours, and I fully expect you to barge in if we go over one minute."

"Understood. Don't worry, I will save you from Jack's clutches."

"I will be forever grateful," I say as I wipe another wave of sweat from my forehead.

"It's no problem. I don't really like the man, either. But let's get back to the office so Gemma doesn't die out here in the heat," Nick says.

"All right," Brittany agrees.

"Thanks, Nick," I reply.

He smiles and says, "Anytime."

Again, I follow behind them as we walk back to the building through the thick and disgusting air. For once, I am actually happy to be in the building when the air-conditioned air starts to dry the sweat and allows me to breathe more easily. I have almost stopped sweating when I get back to my desk.

"See you at the monthly," Nick says as he passes back to his own cube.

Ugh. Don't remind me. I hate that stupid meeting.

You hate all meetings.

True. But not all meetings have the entire department in there to watch me look like a fool.

No one is watching you. And what happened to your positive self-talk? Stacey would be so disappointed. You haven't been to see her in weeks. Get back to your self-talk. It may help.

It's okay to not be perfect. Yeah, I've said that many times, and I still don't believe it. I wish my medication was working. I still feel like a hot mess whenever I am in meetings. It's not fair.

You don't have to be perfect.

Yeah. I know. I wish knowing that fact helped.

Just breathe. Keep your head above water. You will be fine.

Thirty minutes fly by as I pretend to look busy. I get up five minutes early, so that I can get a good seat. By good seat, I mean the farthest in the back that I can go without falling out of a window or merging myself with a wall.

If only.

I am the first one here, per usual. The department is too big for everyone to be able to sit around the table, so I claim an overflow chair that is sitting against the wall and in the back corner.

Normal people probably would sit at the table if they got here first.

I think I've established that I am not normal. I won't talk, anyway. It's best if I am in the back trying to achieve invisibility. If anyone can willingly or unwillingly become invisible, I am sure it's me.

People begin to file into the room. Carl takes a seat at the table, logs onto the computer, and pulls up slides on the large television screen along the wall. Barb sits next to Carl. Ed and Nick sit next to each other at the table and instantly begin to whisper to one another. Before long, all the seats have been taken.

"Okay," Carl starts. "I can't believe it's already been a month since our last meeting."

"I can," Ed says under his breath.

Carl laughs. "Yes, I guess a lot has happened in the last month."

I feel my body tense and my breathing begins to speed up. My head gets light, and my stomach turns.

No. You are not supposed to do this anymore. You are supposed to be better.

But I'm not. I look down at my pad of paper and start scribbling words down. My ears start to ring. I feel like I might pass out.

Why are you doing this? The meeting has barely started. It's not like he has mentioned…

"Bookroll," Carl says.

I physically jump.

Shit. You are so weird.

I overcompensate by moving around in my chair and switching my legs that are crossed. Maybe no one noticed.

Oh, they noticed.

Shut up. I cannot hear anything that is being said. I can only hear my heartbeat and the rush of blood to my head.

Calm down. Calm down right this instant. This is not cool. Calm down.

But I don't. I am in hell. This feeling is physical torture. I can't explain it to someone who has never felt it, but it is its own kind of physical, mental, and emotional torture. I will not be able to calm myself down for the entirety of the meeting, and I know it. There is no stopping the unstoppable beast.

I can feel tears starting to well up in my eyes.

Don't you dare. Breathe in. One. Two. Three. Breathe out. One. Two. Three. And again.

Don't you dare do this, Gemma. You can make it through this meeting. You always do. Just hold on a little while longer.

I look at my watch. There's forty-five more minutes left to the meeting. I almost whimper.

You are stronger than this! You are!

I don't hear anything that is said the entire meeting, and I have written down nonsensical words and drawn all sorts of shapes and squiggles on my paper. Still in a state of distress when the meeting finally ends, I wait for everyone else to leave the room before I even get up out of my seat.

Why, Gemma? Why? Why do you have to be like this? Why can't you just be normal like everyone else? Why can't you be happy-go-lucky like the rest of your department? Why do the simplest tasks feel like torture to you? Why are you like this?

Instead of going back to my desk, I make a stop at the restroom. I lock myself into a stall and finally let myself cry.

It's okay to not be perfect. It's okay. If being less than perfect is okay, then why do I feel like a failure? Why do I feel like I can't be normal? Why do I feel like life is a struggle for me, but not for anyone else? Why does anxiety take over my body and my mind?

Enough, Gemma. Pull yourself together. You have to get through the rest of the day. You can and you will. You always do. Now, wipe away your tears, stand up straight, take a deep breath, and walk back to your desk like nothing happened, like the badass chick that you are, a warrior princess.

With my eyes staring at the floor, I walk out of the bathroom and back to my desk.

See. You can just hide here in your cube until the day is over. You don't have any more meetings. You will feel better tomorrow. You always do. You will survive. You always do.

Swim. One more time today, Gemma. Just swim.

I take a deep breath and relax my shoulders. Yes, I can swim a little this afternoon. I only have a couple more hours, and then I am free. I am free to go home and curl up on my couch and obsess about every little thing that happened today and all the other days for that matter.

Damn it, Gemma. There is no need to obsess.

Oh, I know that there is no need, but I will anyway. There is no stopping it. It will happen no matter what. It will happen tonight and every other night for the rest of my life.

Okay. Can you not obsess now, at least? Can you just stare blankly at your computer for the rest of the day and pretend like you are on a tropical beach somewhere sipping mai tais?

I don't exactly wish myself away to paradise, but I do get some work finished before the day is over. Not even waiting one second longer than I have to, I get up at 5 o'clock on the dot, lock my computer, and speed walk down to the elevators with my eyes focused on the floor. The elevator doors open, and I walk in with two people who were faster than I was at running away today. We ride down to the lobby in silence.

Walking briskly to the door, I am almost free, when I remember that I told McGruff that I would walk to Sally's with him after work. I immediately stop and pace next to the wall.

Do I just go? Do I wait? I can't wait here any longer. My coworkers will start to come down, and I can't face them. I have to leave.

But before I can, there is a gentle brush on my forearm. I turn to see McGruff standing next to me.

"You beat me," he says.

"Yeah, I had to get out of there. I ran right out at five."

"I'm glad I did, too. It looked like you were going to pace right out of here if I didn't come along quickly."

"No comment."

He smiles. "Well, shall we then?"

I follow him out of the lobby and into the blazing heat of the afternoon. My forehead starts to sweat the second the sun hits my skin.

"So gross," I say.

"I know I am, but you don't have to say it all the time."

He is so cute sometimes. My lips curve into a smile and my shoulders relax a little.

"I like to remind you, to keep you humble."

"How was your day?"

"Ugh. I have to set up recurring meetings with Jack and meet with him all by myself."

"Why?"

"Because Carl wants me to, so I can finish my requirements sooner rather than later."

"Sounds like a form of abuse."

"It is! I told Nick that he has to save me and barge into our meeting if we run late."

"Save you?"

"Yeah, I have to set up meetings with him, too, so I set it up right after my meeting with Jack."

"So he can save you."

Yes. What's not to understand?

"Yes. I told Nick that he had to, and he agreed."

"Oh," he says and turns his head away from me.

"If it's even possible, it seems hotter now than it did at lunch."

"At lunch?" he asks and turns back in my direction.

"Yeah. I went to the park."

"You went *out* at lunch?"

"Yes."

"How was it?"

"Disgusting."

"I am surprised you went out. You seemed miserable at the Common this weekend."

"Yeah. I was. But they were very persuasive."

"They?"

"Brittany and Nick."

"Nick? The guy that you have to meet with?"

"Yeah."

"I thought he was older, like Jack's age."

"No. He's our age."

"Do you go out to lunch with them a lot?"

"It's usually just Brittany, but she's gotten closer to him in the daily meeting."

"Oh, so you don't really know him?"

"I do. He sits on the other side of the partition from me. Before Brittany, he was probably my best work friend."

"Your work husband?"

"What? No. He's just a coworker."

"He was in the daily meetings with you?"

"Yeah, why?"

"You've just never talked about him before."

"There wasn't much to talk about."

"You said he was your work husband."

"No. You said that."

He doesn't respond, and we walk in silence for the rest of the way to Sally's.

Please let Walter be there. Please let Walter be there.

McGruff holds the door open for me, and I see Walter sitting by the window. He is in his eighties and, like usual, wearing a polo shirt and khakis.

Yes!

I head straight over and sit down next to him. McGruff follows suit.

"Hey, kid. How're you, today?" Walter asks.

"I'm good. How are you?"

"Not too bad myself. Nate?"

"I am fine."

Fine? What is his deal? Why is he cranky pants all of a sudden? He does not seem fine.

"Hey, huns," Sally says from behind the counter. "What can I get for you, today?"

"I recommend the casserole. Superb," Walter offers.

"I'll have the casserole, Sally," McGruff says.

"And you, Gem?"

"Same thing. Thanks, Sally."

"Be right up."

"What's new, Walter?" McGruff asks. "I haven't seen you around lately."

"Actually, my son just booked a flight to come out and see me in a couple of weeks."

"Wow! That's great, Walter!" I say.

"Oh, that is great. How long is he staying?" McGruff asks.

"About a week. I don't know what I am going to do with him for that long."

Walter laughs and winks at me.

"I'm sure you will think of something," McGruff says.

"Even if you don't do anything, I'm sure it will be perfect," I say.

"I am sure Josh will have something in mind," Walter says.

"Is your granddaughter coming?" Sally asks as she puts down two plates of casserole in front of me and McGruff.

"No, not this time."

"Hopefully, next time then."

After eating my meal, I look at McGruff, who hasn't made eye contact with me since we got here. He is staring down at his, now empty, plate.

Ask if he's okay.

No. He clearly isn't.

Which is why you should ask.

I reach over and grab his forearm. "Is everything okay?" I ask.

"Sure," he responds.

So, no. He really means no.

"Okay, well, Walter, I am going home," I say. "I will see you later. Nate, do you want to walk out with me?"

"No. I am going to stay here with Walter for a little while. Besides, you aren't a damsel in distress, right? I am sure you will be fine. You don't need me to save you."

What the heck?

"Right. Okay. Bye."

CHAPTER THREE

It's Friday night. I have canceled on my therapist Stacey, again. I am lying flat on the couch with my face smushed against the seat cushion while I watch my phone buzz on the coffee table in front of me for the fifth time. Groggily, I flop my hand over to my phone and pick it up. The texts are all from Brittany.

"You're going to be there, right?"

"You're coming, right?"

"Gemma?"

"You'd better be getting ready."

"You have to go with me."

Why do I befriend people like this?

You don't. They befriend you.

Ugh. I shouldn't let them.

One more text: "You're going."

Tonight is our work party at Fenway Park. I guess I am going.

Yes. It will be good for you. Get your butt up off the couch. You need to get ready.

Ready? I need to change?

What? You're just going to wear what you wore to work?

Yes.

No. Everyone already saw you in that.

So? They've seen all of my clothes. I go there every day.

Put in a little effort, will you? It's a party. It's time to celebrate all those months you spent getting P2 up and running.

What I like to call The Period of Great Sadness.

No, don't think like that. This is supposed to be fun.

Since when are work parties fun?

Well, with that attitude, it won't be.

One more text from Brittany: "Gemma!!!!!!!"

You need to text her back, or she is going to have a mental breakdown.

Fine.

And tell her you are going.

Ugh. Fine.

I type out, "Yes, I will be there. Meet you outside the gate."

Damn it. Now, I definitely have to go.

Yes. Now get your lazy butt up off of the couch and put on a nice summer dress.

Why?

Just do it.

And I do. I pull up my Road Trip app on my phone, call a car, and head down to the lobby to wait for the red Ford Taurus to pull up in front of me. Opening the door, I get into the back seat. I close the door, and the driver grunts.

"You're going to Fenway?" He sounds disgusted and doesn't even look at me when he speaks, not even in the mirror. He pulls away from the curb before I can answer.

"Yes."

"You're lucky there's not a game tonight, the traffic would be horrible. I wouldn't be able to get you close to the gate. What are you doing there, anyway?"

Like it's any of your business.

"My company is having a party for us."

"Oh yeah? Where in the park?"

"The Sam Deck."

"Oh man! I love the deck! It has a great view of the field. You're going to love it. Too bad there isn't a game tonight!"

So, which is it? I'm lucky there's not a game tonight or too bad there isn't one?

I look out the window as the Taurus merges onto Storrow Drive. I watch as we pass the Esplanade on the right, or the Hat Shell, where the Boston Pops play during the Fourth of July fireworks. The car

38

drives parallel to the Charles River, and I can see a few sailboats on the water. Crowds of people are walking and running alongside the water's edge. It is a gorgeous summer night.

I'm glad that I'm doing this.

What? Did you really just think that? Don't be glad yet. You're not there yet.

What are you doing to me? Do you want me to get anxious? Because you know I will!

My heartbeat starts to speed up.

No! No. No. You're fine. You can do this. This will be fun. It's a beautiful summer night. It's not raining. It's not too cold. It's perfect.

"All right. Here we are at Gate B," the driver says.

What? Already? That came out of nowhere.

As the car turns to the left, I can see the park from the window. The Taurus pulls to the curb and stops.

"Have fun up there tonight."

"Thank you. I will."

That was optimistic.

Shut up.

Getting out of the car, I look up at the red brick walls and the green stands. I didn't expect the park to be so pretty.

"Hey!" Brittany waves to me.

She is sitting on the ledge in front of four statues of baseball players holding baseball bats. "Teammates" is engraved in the stone block.

"You made it!"

"Of course, I did."

Please. It's never an "of course" with you.

"I'm excited. This is going to be fun!"

"Me too."

Holy crap. I meant that. I *am* excited. How did I let this happen?

"Have you ever been here before?" she asks.

"No. Never. I don't really have a reason to come down here. Have you?"

"Yeah. I've been to a few games."

Of course, she has. She is super cool. Why did she ever befriend me?

She took pity on you.

Shut up.

"Should we go in?" she asks.

No. Is that an option?

"Yeah."

A stadium employee is standing right inside the gate.

"Are you here with KPM Insurance?" she asks.

"Yes, we are," Brittany answers.

"Great. Just go up those stairs to my right. Food and drinks are available at the concession stand and all are being paid for by KPM, so enjoy."

Brittany looks at me and smiles.

"Thank you!" she yells over her shoulder at the park employee as we walk towards the green staircase. "Free food and booze? I can't believe it! This is great!"

"Yeah. It is."

Holy crap. I meant that. It really is great.

See, you're feeling better already.

Don't push it.

As we ascend the stairs, the music from the deck gets louder and louder. When we reach the top, I see that we are a couple of the last people to arrive. Coworkers are already drinking and eating at the standup tables or at the booths with umbrellas. Everyone is smiling and laughing. I look over at Brittany, who is practically glowing with excitement.

Damn. Her last company must have sucked if she thinks this is fun.

"Come on. Let's get some beer," she says.

We get our free beer and walk out from underneath the overhang to a full view of the field.

Holy crap. This is beautiful. I didn't expect it to be so nice in here. The grass is perfectly manicured, bright green, with two socks cut into the outfield. The empty seats around the field are bright red and a perfect contrast to the green field and the green metal support beams. The iconic Green Monster, or left field wall, is to my right, and the Fenway Park sign is all the way across the field on the front of the offices and radio booths for broadcasters. The lights over the field are lit, and it's like it's the middle of the day. The field is so bright and illuminated. It's gorgeous.

"Gemma, what do you think?"

"I didn't expect it to be so..."

"Pretty?"

"Exactly."

"Hey ladies!" Nick appears behind us. "I've been waiting for you two to show up. I'm going to grab some food and then head down to one of those tables overlooking the field. Care to join?"

"Yes!" Brittany agrees immediately.

They both turn to look at me.

Oh, I have to answer, too?

Yes, you do. Say yes.

"Yes."

We gather our beer, fill our plates with food, and head down a few steps into what is sort of a platform jutting out over the stands below. It is lined with green tables and chairs. Nick and Brittany sit on opposite sides of the table. I sit next to Brittany.

"You look really pretty. That's a nice dress," Nick says to me.

"Thanks. You can borrow it if you want."

They both laugh.

What the hell, Gemma? He can borrow it? First, no he can't. Second, why would you say that? Of course, he doesn't want to borrow it. It would never fit.

Just pretend like it never happened.

"It's really nice of KPM to do this for us," Nick says.

"I agree," Brittany replies. "And I've been meaning to ask this, what does KPM stand for? No one told me."

Nick looks at me and then Brittany does.

"Turner Classic Movies?"

Brittany laughs. "I think that's TCM."

"Then, yeah. I don't know."

Brittany and I look at Nick.

"If Gemma doesn't know, then I sure as hell don't."

"Well, the company I worked for before this never would have done this for us. I've never been to a work party before."

"Yeah," I say, "this one sets the bar too high. It shouldn't have been the first you went to. They are mostly a lot worse than this."

"Worse?" she inquires.

"Don't let Gemma cloud your thoughts about work parties," Nick says. "They aren't so bad. Gemma just hates socializing."

So? What's the big deal with that?

"No," I counter, "they aren't all at Fenway. They are usually at some hotel function room, and we are stuck talking to people we don't want to because the whole company is there crammed into one little space. And the VPs mingle around like they are just common folk. It's not natural."

"They're not so bad," Nick adds.

"Ugh." I roll my eyes and groan as Jack and Bill sit down at the table next to ours. "You were saying?"

"What do you say, we go down into the stands?" Nick suggests.

"Is that allowed?" Brittany asks.

"I don't see why not."

"You want us to jump down into the stands from here?" I ask.

Nick smiles. "No, silly. We go over there and walk down the stairs."

He points behind us.

"Oh."

Oh my God, Gemma. Are you for real? Did you really just ask that? Did you really think he wanted you to jump down from here? So embarrassing.

Stopping for more beer first, the three of us walk down into the middle of an aisle under the overhang and overlooking right field. Nick first, then Brittany, and then me. We position ourselves in the center of the row and sit in the red seats.

"Have you guys been to a game before?" Nick asks.

"I've been to a few," Brittany responds.

"What about you, Gemma?"

"No. I haven't."

"We should go sometime, then," Nick says. After a couple of seconds, he adds, "All of us."

"Yeah, that would be fun," Brittany answers.

"How long have you been a fan?" Nick asks her.

"Just recently, after they started to win."

"Oh! So, you're a pink hat."

"I don't know what that means."

"Are you one too, Gemma?"

"It sounds like you hate them. So, yeah I'm probably one."

Nick smiles. "Are you a fan of baseball, Gemma?"

"No."

"Then you're not a pink hat. But Brittany here definitely is."

"Hey! I don't know what you're talking about, but I can tell it's not a good thing."

Nick laughs. "It's a bandwagon fan. You buy a pink Red Sox hat instead of the traditional blue hat and red 'B.' And you are a fan only because they started to win. You didn't suffer through decades of losing like the rest of us."

"Oh, then yeah. I probably am," Brittany whispers.

"That's right. You should be ashamed."

"Yeah, thanks." Brittany smiles.

"So, Gemma, since you've never been here, that post right there," he points to a tall yellow pole at the edge of the stands on our left, "that's Pesky Pole."

"Pesky Pole?" I ask.

"Yes. It's the foul pole. It's named after Johnny Pesky."

Oh, right, of course.

"And that, over there," he points to our right, "is the Green Monster."

"I know what that is!" I shout.

"Okay, okay. Didn't know what you knew. Now, I do."

We sit for a few minutes, sipping our beers and looking out over the park.

Actually, this is pretty nice. It has to be the best work party I've been to.

"I don't mean to bring it up," Brittany says. "But, Carl mentioned that you'd be rejoining us soon in the pit of despair?"

"Yeah. He told me by the end of the month. So, I only have another week before I have to return to the shit storm."

"Well, if it's any consolation," Nick says, "we do miss you."

"Please," I say. "As if you'd stop chatting with Ed long enough to realize I'm not there."

"Oh!" Brittany screeches. "So true! She's got you there."

Nick squints his eyes. "So what if I have a bromance with Ed? I've got to make it through that meeting alive somehow."

I sigh. "Truer words have never been spoken," I say.

Brittany nods. "Agreed." She looks at me. "But still, he probably didn't notice you were gone until I just mentioned it."

"Hey!" Nick shouts.

"She got you," I say.

Nick shakes his head and takes a sip of his beer. We all lean back in our seats and look out over the meticulously groomed field and empty stands all around us. This is actually quite a sight. I never thought that this party would be so much fun.

We all turn around in our seats as a giant roar and cheer comes up from the Sam Deck.

"What was that?" Brittany asks.

"This is the point in time at a work party when things start to deteriorate," I say.

"Deteriorate?" she asks.

"Should we just go back up and let her see for herself?" Nick asks me.

I nod. "It's the only way to fully appreciate the experience."

"Should I be scared?" Brittany asks. "I'm scared."

"Oh, you definitely should be scared," Nick says.

Brittany's eyes open wide, and she looks at me.

"Don't worry," I say. "We will protect you."

"But if you want to join in, I'm not stopping you," Nick says.

"Join in what?" Brittany asks.

"Okay. It's time to show her," I say.

The three of us stand up and walk out of the row and up the stairs to the loud music and cheers of the Sam Deck. When we reach the top, we stop, and I hear Brittany gasp. She puts her hands up over her mouth.

"Yep," Nick says.

"I never wanted to see this," Brittany says.

No one does.

Fred is in the middle of the deck dancing with a couple of web programmers, and a circle has formed around them. We are just in time to witness Barb push through the circle into the middle to dance with Fred.

"Oh, my God," Brittany says. "I can't tell if I'm excited, feel awkward, or am extremely embarrassed for them."

"Yeah. It's a range of emotions," I say.

"Look at Bob," Nick says to us.

We all turn to see Bob's shocked, maybe disgusted, reaction before he drops back into professional VP mode.

You should go say hi to Bob. Show him that you came and are thankful for the party.

No. Heck no. Why would I voluntarily do that?

Go say hi.

No!

Bob backs slowly away from the crowd, looks in all directions, and then starts to walk our way.

No. Please no. I know we look like the only normal people here right now, but please don't come over here.

But he does.

"Hi, guys. How are you all? Having fun?" Bob asks.

"Yes, we are," Brittany answers.

Thank goodness for Brittany. I never have to do any of the heavy lifting in conversations with her.

"Good. I'm glad. I'm happy you could all come out. It's a beautiful night."

The VPs pretending to be one of us and making small talk is probably one of the biggest reasons I hate work parties. We know he has nothing to say to us. He knows that we know. But we all must stand here and do this dance until he realizes there is nothing left to say, and he slowly walks away in an awkward silence while we all make those polite half smiles and wish this never happened.

"Are you already working on P3?" Bob asks.

"Oh, yes," Nick takes this one. "We started right away after go-live."

"You all did such a great job. I was happy to put this together for everyone."

"Yes, thank you!" Brittany answers.

And this is it, the end of the line for the small talk. Cue the half smiles, Bob nodding, and now slowly backing away and walking towards some other unsuspecting group. I let out a huge breath.

You didn't talk to him at all, Gemma.

So? I smiled and nodded. Brittany and Nick did just fine.

Goodness gracious, Gemma. If you want people and Bob to think you are normal, you have to act normal.

If I could, I would. At least, I'm not in the middle of the floor dancing with Fred and Barb.

Thank God for that.

"You ladies want to dance?" Nick asks.

"No!" Brittany and I both yell at the same time.

Nick laughs. We all look over as Carl uncomfortably squeezes in between two people in the circle and walks into the middle to break up Barb and Fred dancing a little too close for comfort. Brittany makes a face.

"Okay, how about we get out of there then? This is about the time when everyone starts to leave because of the pure awkwardness. What do you say we go to the Cask 'n Flagon?"

"Oh!" Brittany shouts. "How about the Lansdowne Pub? They have live music!" She claps her hands.

"I am up for that," Nick says.

They both turn to look at me.

Me, again? Ugh. I can say no, right?

No. You have to go. What are you going to do? Go home and curl up on your couch?

Yes.

It's Friday night, and it's not even nine o'clock.

So?

So, you should go.

"I guess, I could be persuaded to go, too," I say.

"Yes!" Brittany says.

"Okay, we just have to go out this gate because I don't think any of the others are open right now and walk down and around to the other side of the park to Lansdowne Street."

"Walk?" Brittany asks.

"Yeah. It's not that far. And it's not that scary, I promise. If anything happens, I will save you."

"Both of us?" I ask.

"No, just Brittany. You are on your own, Gemma."

"Okay, good," I respond. "I've been looking for a reason to try out my Tae Bo moves."

"Tae Bo?" Nick asks. "How long have you been waiting to try those out?"

"Ah, twenty years maybe."

"You will probably be a little rusty. I guess, I can save you, too."

I smirk.

We make our way out of the gate and around the corner to Lansdowne Street. I can hear the music before we even get to the door.

"Should we sit inside or out?" Nick asks.

Oh, please inside in the air conditioning.

"Inside so we can hear the music," Brittany responds.

Oh, thank goodness!

"Gemma, that okay with you?" Nick asks.

"Yep."

The inside has a pub-like feel, but it is a lot nicer than Flannery's. It's like an upscale pub with high top chairs at the bar, a long table across the room kind of like a second bar where you sit next to strangers, booths against the walls, and dark wooden tables in the middle of the room. There is a little stage with a band with three members currently playing on it—a drummer, a bassist, and a vocalist also playing guitar.

I follow Nick and Brittany to one of the tables in the middle and sit down. We all order a round of beer and watch the band.

"How was your first work party, Brittany?" Nick asks.

"It was quite interesting. It was more fun than I expected, but also more awkward. I did not expect dancing."

"Yeah. No one really expects or wants it, but it somehow always happens," I say.

"You should have been there the time Gemma danced," Nick says.

I glare at Nick.

"I don't believe that for one second," Brittany says.

"You shouldn't," I say.

See, this isn't so bad, is it? You are just hanging out with two of your coworkers after the work party. It's completely normal. There was no reason not to come. You aren't even anxious.

Yeah, I guess it's not that bad, except I have nothing to talk about. I don't know much about them on a personal level. We probably don't have much in common besides work.

Well, why don't you ask?

Ask? Me? No. I don't ask things. I just sit and listen.

Listen? Really? What have they been talking about?

Crap. Why do I always forget to listen?

"Gemma, what do you think about Carl?" Nick asks.

"Carl? He's not terrible."

Brittany laughs. "Wow, what a resounding endorsement that was."

"I don't think he is terrible either" Nick says. "He isn't the worst boss. I would much rather have him as my boss than Barb."

"Oh, my God. I would quit if Barb became my boss," I say.

"What do you have against Barb?" Brittany asks. "I don't really interact with her at all."

"Has she ever hip checked you into a wall? Because she does that to me all the time," I answer.

Nick laughs. "She does that to me, too! I was thinking I should start to wear protective padding into work, just in case I run into her. Literally."

"She sounds great," Brittany replies.

"She is a notch below Jack," I say.

"On your hit list?" Nick asks.

"How did you know?" I ask.

"Just a hunch."

49

Jack! I had completely forgotten for a moment that I had to meet with him one-on-one. Multiple times. Ugh. Why did I have to bring up Jack? Now, I will obsess about it all night and all weekend.

Girl, you were going to do that, anyway.

"Another round?" Nick asks.

"Not for me," I say. "I'm too tired."

"Too much excitement at the work party. What about you, Brittany?"

"I think I'm going to call it a night, too. Sorry, Nick."

"Ah, no worries. I was pushing my luck hanging out with two beautiful ladies for so long, anyway."

"Yeah, yeah," Brittany says.

I pull my wallet out of my purse, and Brittany does the same.

"Nope," Nick says. "My treat."

"That's not necessary," I say.

"No, let us pay," Brittany adds.

But Nick swipes the bill off the table and walks over to the bar without our money.

I look at Brittany. She shrugs.

"That's nice of him," she says.

Standing, we wait a couple of minutes for Nick to return, and we all walk out together. Brittany's car arrives first.

"See you two Monday," she says as she climbs into the back of the sedan.

"That was fun," Nick says as we watch Brittany's Road Trip drive into the distance.

"Yeah, it was. Thanks for paying."

"Oh, no worries. I like you, guys."

I smile as my Road Trip pulls up before us. Taking a step forward, I turn when Nick grabs my arm just above the wrist. I furrow my brow.

"You okay?" I ask.

What the heck?

"Yeah," he says and immediately drops my arm. "Sorry."

I tilt my head to the left. "Okay…"

"See you, Monday," he murmurs.

"Yep." I squint at him, and he takes a couple of steps back.

Odd. What was that?

I get into the car, close the door, and look out the window as the car pulls away. Nick is still standing there watching me with that confused look on his face.

What is up with him?

CHAPTER FOUR

It's 8:43 in the morning. I am lying in bed staring at the ceiling and have been for at least an hour, probably more, when my phone buzzes.

What the crap? Who is texting me at this time?

I lift the phone up over my face without sitting up.

It's McGruff. "I know it's Saturday," the text reads, "but I was wondering if you and Liz want to come to O'Brady's with me and my friends tonight? We didn't get to see each other last night because of your work party."

I lie the phone down on my chest and close my eyes. Do I want to go? I don't think so. But I should, right?

Yes, you should want to go.

I don't even want to go out with Liz, though. Can I just cancel on both of them?

Again? No, you can't do that. You have to go out. Look at you. You are lying in bed and haven't moved even though you've been wide awake for hours.

So?

So, you need to see people. You need to get out of your apartment. You need to see the guy you are dating. You need to see your best friend.

Can't I just stay in?

No.

Can't I *just* see my best friend?

No. You should go to O'Brady's.

Picking the phone up off of my chest, I again hover it over my face and start a text to Liz.

"Do you want to maybe go to O'Brady's tonight instead of Flannery's? Nate invited you and me to hang out with his friends."

Please say, no. Please say, no.

"Why don't you just go without me?" she responds.

What? No. She was supposed to say that I should just hang with her like usual.

"No, you're the cool, funny one."

"You'll be fine."

"Come with me, please? Or we can just go to Flannery's like usual, just the two of us, and forget about O'Brady's."

"No, I will go with you. Just don't cancel on us both at the last minute."

There goes my backup plan.

"Okay. Want to meet at Flannery's for one before we go? I don't want to show up there alone. And a little buzz would help me out."

"Sure, I will meet you at Flannery's, regular time."

"You're the best," I tell her.

"I know."

Shit. Maybe I can convince her to stay with me at Flannery's.

What is the deal here? Do you not want to see McGruff?

I reply to McGruff, "Sure. We will meet you at O'Brady's tonight."

"Great!" he replies. "I will see you then!"

What do I reply? What do I reply?

Whatever you do, don't just send a smiley face.

Damn it. You just sent a smiley face.

I didn't know what to respond.

Fine. But you have to go. There is no getting out of this. You cannot pretend to be sick.

Ugh. Fine.

You should get out of bed, though.

Shut up.

But I do. I roll out of bed and move to the couch where I remain for the rest of the day.

You are such a sloth. Couldn't you have done something productive today?

Like what?

Anything but sit on the couch all day.

Maybe I should just sit on the couch all night, too. Why should I ruin a good thing by going out? I have nothing to say or talk about anyway. I don't feel like going out. I should just do us all a favor and stay in. They probably secretly want me to, anyway. I know I am getting on both of their nerves. They will probably thank me for staying in. And if I don't, we will all regret it.

For the love of all things good in this world, get your lazy ass off of the couch, put some clothes on, and go meet your best friend for a drink.

Rude.

And don't forget to brush your hair.

Like they would even care if I don't brush it.

But I do. I change my clothes and even brush my teeth before walking down to the lobby to wait for my Road Trip. The car drops me off in front of Flannery's, and I step onto the curb and stand there as the car rolls away behind me.

Am I really doing this?

Yes. You are here. It is stupid if you go home now.

I am prepared to be stupid.

"Hey, Gemma."

Oh, shit. I've been spotted.

I turn to see Barry strolling down the sidewalk.

"Hey, Barry."

"Going in?"

No.

But he doesn't wait for me to answer, he is already holding the door open for me.

Shitty shit shit.

What is your deal tonight? Are you anxious about talking to McGruff's friends, or do you not want to see McGruff?

I can't tell. I can't tell what I am feeling lately.

I walk through the door, and the air conditioning cools my face. I hadn't even noticed how much I was sweating.

"Hey, Liz," I say as I sit down next to her.

"I am glad you made it."

"Shut up. I was here last week."

"True."

"Usual?" Greg asks.

"Yes, please."

Greg nods and walks over to Barry, who has taken a seat at the other end of the bar.

"What's up with Barry?" I ask. "He didn't even try to talk to us."

Liz shrugs. "Maybe he's just sober."

"I think that's exactly it," Greg says as he places my drink in front of me and walks away again.

Liz turns to look at me. "So, O'Brady's? Have you been back since you just ran out that one time?"

"Okay, that is harsh, but true. And no, I haven't. That's why I needed you to come tonight. You are more talkative, and his friends will like you way more than they like me."

"That is not true."

"It's so true. And you will at least try to keep me from running away again."

"I will try, but I usually can't control you."

"I know. But I am glad that you are here. I would feel awkward going over there alone after I dashed out of there the last time."

"It must have been a weird first impression."

"Yeah, I can't imagine why they would want me to come back. Nate must have invited me without their knowledge."

"I doubt that. I am sure they didn't even notice anything weird last time."

"I disappeared."

"I am sure Nate told them that you had to leave."

"I guess."

See, I should have said no to McGruff and just stayed here with Liz, like usual on Saturday. This is going to be horrible. His friends must think I am so weird. I shouldn't go over there. I should stay here.

Okay, Ms. McGruff is coming back out.

"Any chance you want to just stay here?" I ask.

"No! We are not canceling on Nate."

"Any chance *you* just want to go over, and I can stay here?"

"No! We are both going, and that is final."

"Where are you two going?" Greg asks.

"Across the street," Liz says. "Can we get our check?"

"Already?" he asks. "You just got here."

"Yeah. We are meeting Gemma's guy and his friends."

"Oh!" Greg shouts. "Make sure to tell me all about it next week."

"We are really going?" I ask.

"Yes."

She pushes out her chair, stands, and waits for me to do the same.

I can hold my ground, I know it. I think Greg will be on my side.

Stand up, Gemma.

And I do. I wave to Greg as we leave the bar, look both ways, and scurry across Boylston Street while the traffic is clear. We stop on the curb.

"Are they all going to be there?" Liz asks.

"I am assuming so."

"You ready?"

"No. Can we go back?"

Liz tucks a strand of hair behind her ear. "No."

"You hesitated. That means we can go back."

"No. We can do this. We have each other."

"Okay. Just don't leave me."

"I won't."

Liz opens the door, and a wave of cool air and laughter rolls out of the pub. She braves her way in, and I follow.

Why did I agree to come here? I should have just said no.

Well, it's too late for that now. Look at you. You are here. Try to be friendly.

Liz has led me right to them. McGruff turns around and smiles at us.

"Hey! I am glad you made it," he says. "Nice to see you again, Liz."

"You too."

He maneuvers next to me, puts his arm around my waist, and kisses the top of my head.

"Guys, you remember Gemma, right? And this is her friend, Liz. Liz, this is John." He points to a tall and lanky red head who waves at us. "And this is Dan. We work together at Digitize Tech." McGruff motions to a shorter, but more muscular, man with brown hair and dimples on both cheeks. "This guy right here is George. I also work with him." A man with a round face and freckles on his nose gives us the thumbs up. "And finally, Pete." Pete looks like a jock, with his blonde crew cut and broad shoulders.

"What have we missed?" Liz asks.

"Not a whole lot," Dan offers. "We were just boring John and Pete with software engineering talk. There's a conference in California coming up that Nate…"

"That I was geeking out over," McGruff interrupts.

"Right." Dan replies. "It sounds pretty cool. I wish I got to go."

"See," Pete says. "So boring. I am glad you two are here now."

"I am not sure we are much more interesting," Liz says.

"Oh," John says. "Anything is better than a discussion on the latest code that these three have been working on."

"If you only knew how cool it is," George replies.

"Anyway," John says. "How are you doing, Gemma? We haven't seen you in a while."

"I am good. I've just been working and staying in a lot."

"Grown sick of our Nate, already, huh?" Pete asks.

"No, not completely, anyway." I grin up at McGruff.

"Give it time," George says. "It will happen soon."

"Hey!" McGruff shouts. "I thought you guys would be on my side, here. And I find out that you are secretly betting against me?"

"Would you really expect anything less from us?" George asks.

"We definitely bet against Pete when he met his girlfriend," John says.

"What!" Pete shouts.

"You know we did. She is so much cooler than you are," George says.

"I know she is, but come on, guys," Pete says.

"And she's better looking," John adds.

"Whoa!" Pete reacts.

The three of them continue to taunt each other as McGruff squares off and turns so that he, Liz, and I are in a circle of our own.

"Sorry about them," he says.

"They're great," Liz says.

"Yeah, I like them," I reply.

Good, you said something instead of just standing there like a moron, even if what you said was a lie.

It wasn't a lie. I do like them.

"Hey, how was Fenway last night?" Liz asks.

"Oh, yeah," McGruff adds. "How was it?"

"It was actually really fun. They had free food and drinks and music pumping."

"Did they do mixed drinks there?" Liz asks.

"No. I had beer."

"You drink beer?" Liz asks.

"You drink beer?" McGruff echoes.

"Why is that so surprising?"

"I just haven't seen you drink beer before," Liz says.

"Yeah, well all the cool kids were doing it," I say.

"Brittany?" McGruff asks.

"Yeah. And Nick."

"You hung out with Nick, too?"

Why does he seem so surprised? Can he not believe that I have more than one friend?

"Yeah. We actually went down into the stands to sit for a while. It was cool."

"Just the three of you?" McGruff asks.

"Yeah. We even went out after, too."

Surprised, Liz asks, "You went out after?"

Why do they both seem stunned? It's not like I am a complete loser. Am I?

You shouldn't ask such questions.

So, I've canceled on them the last couple of weeks. That doesn't mean that I don't like going out.

But you don't. You honestly don't.

Not all the time, no. But sometimes. I am here, aren't I?

Yes. But you didn't want to be.

Shut up.

"Where did you guys go?" Liz asks.

"The Lansdowne Pub. They had a band playing."

"Who are you right now?" Liz asks.

Again, why are they so surprised? Brittany made me go out. The two of them make me go out all of the time. Case in point, I am here.

"Did you call a Road Trip and just leave them there?" McGruff asks.

I can't tell if he is bitter. He seems bitter. He has a tone about him.

"No. We all left at the same time."

"So, I'm the only one you do that to."

Why is he being so grumpy? He is so stereotypical McGruff right now.

I look over at Liz, and she opens her eyes wide as if to say, 'Yikes.'

Okay, at least, I'm not the only one who thinks he's being rude at the moment.

"I don't mean to do that," I say.

"Yeah," he says curtly and turns his back on us to talk with John and George.

I take a few steps out of earshot and say to Liz, "What the hell was that?"

"I don't know."

"Did I say or do something?"

"Not that I saw."

"Sure, I've been kind of cranky lately, but I thought I was fine tonight."

"Yeah. I thought you were in a good mood. You even talked to his friends."

"I know!"

"He'll cool off and be fine."

"I hope so. I don't know what his deal is today."

"Do you think he's jealous of Nick?"

"What? No. There's nothing to be jealous of."

"I know that, but does he? He got a little weird when you mentioned that you hung out with Nick last night."

"Brittany was there, too."

"You have been hanging out with Nick a lot lately."

"At work! And with Brittany! We are coworkers. He literally sits next to me all day."

"Why are you getting so defensive?"

Yeah, why are you?

"I'm not. I'm just saying that Nate can't be mad that I hang out with my coworkers at work and at work parties. Look at him. He's got two coworkers with him right now. And he hangs out with them all the time, every Saturday. It's not like I do that."

They did mention going out again and going to a Red Sox game.

Not a good time to bring that up. Let's just keep that quiet for now.

"I know. I'm on your side, Gem," Liz says.

I sigh. "Should we just run across the street and go back to Flannery's? I don't think they'd even miss us at this point."

Liz shakes her head. "No."

"You're no fun. Fine. What are we going to do? Just hang out in the corner until he notices that we are still here?"

"There are worse things than talking to your best friend."

"Ain't that the truth."

Liz and I slowly back away from the group until we are a good distance away from them. A couple is just vacating a table, so we swoop in and take it as they leave. I can finally breathe again. It is just me and my best friend. I can deal with this.

"Do you think they'll mind that we are over here?" Liz asks.

"I doubt they will even notice. They have probably already forgotten that we were even here."

"Yeah, right."

"Did you see how mad Nate got? I am sure he is glad we aren't over there. He probably wants us to sneak out and not come back. Speaking of, can we?"

"Gemma..."

"Is that a yes? Because that feels like a yes."

"It's not a yes. We can stay here for a little while longer. It's not like we ditched them or anything. He turned his back on us."

"Damn straight." I take a sip of my drink. "I am so glad that you are here. I would have already run out of here and been sitting on my couch by now if you weren't."

"I believe it. Nate's friends are nice, though."

"Yeah, they are."

"Something is up with Nate."

"Yep," is all I say before taking another giant gulp of my drink.

We sit for a while, watch the crowd, and try to figure out who is going into and leaving Flannery's across the street.

"Who do you think that is?" Liz asks as a person comes out of the bar and stands on the curb to smoke.

"By his walk, must be Barry."

"How has he been to you lately?"

"Not bad. He's backed off. He doesn't make uncomfortable comments anymore."

"He probably knows about Nate. And he probably knows he never had a chance with you, poor guy."

"Well, he is twenty-five years older than I am."

"Hey, I am on your side, always. I don't actually want you to date Barry."

"I know. I love you."

"I love you, too."

We both turn to the window again.

"That's Greg," we both say at the same time and laugh.

I lean back in my chair and look out over the bar. McGruff is still chatting with his friends and making big gesticulations as he does. He's not mad at them. Gee, I am really glad I came here to hang out with him tonight. He seems really interested in talking to me. Just then he turns around, looks directly at me for a couple seconds, and then turns back. My heartbeat quickens.

Just calm down. He'll be fine. You will be fine. It will all be fine.

"All right," Liz says after a while.

"No."

"I should go."

"No, you said you wouldn't leave me."

"I'm sorry, but it's getting late. You should stay and have fun."

"Have fun? Have you met me? Have you been here this whole time?"

Liz sighs. "Try to have fun."

"Okay. Wait a second, I will tell Nate that you are leaving. I will walk out with you."

Before I even reach McGruff, I can tell by his rigid body language that he is still mad at me. My heart begins to pound.

It's okay. It's just McGruff. Just tell him that you are walking Liz out. If it goes to shit, then you can call a Road Trip and get the hell out of here like you usually do. Sure, he will be ripshit, but at least you will be gone.

I cautiously tap McGruff on the shoulder, and he looks coolly down at me.

"Liz is leaving. I'm going to walk her out. I will be right back."

"You'd better."

"I will."

You will call a Road Trip, you mean?

What the crap does that mean, you'd better? Or what? What's he going to do?

I follow Liz out into the warm night, and we stand on the sidewalk out front.

"Thanks for coming," I say.

"Anytime. I always have fun with you even if we are sitting in the corner avoiding people. Nate's friends are nice. Are you two okay, though?"

I sigh. "I don't know. Maybe. Maybe not."

"You are not going to jump into my Road Trip, are you?"

I hadn't even thought of that. That is a genius idea. I should definitely do that.

"No."

"I'm serious."

"I know you are. Trust me, I want to, but I am not going to."

"Good. Go back in there and have fun."

"Have fun? Again, have you met me?"

"Yes, I have. And I know it's possible."

I roll my eyes.

"Oh, my car is here." Liz takes a few steps and turns to look at me. "Don't follow me."

"I won't."

She smiles, gets into the car, and closes the door. She waves as the car drives by.

Damn. I have to go back in now.

No. You have options. You can call your own Road Trip. She only said not to get into hers. Or you can run across the street and go to Flannery's.

McGruff told me I'd better be back.

What better way to show him that he can't tell you what to do than to disappear this very instant?

That's a good point. But, no I can't. The last time I was out with his friends, I just hightailed it out of here without even saying goodbye. I can't do that again. I can't do that to McGruff again.

Fine. Then march your tushy back in there and try to be nice. At least, there's air conditioning in there.

There're so many people in there.

It will be fine. Just push your way in and through the crowd back to McGruff. He can't be mad at you all night. Worst case scenario, you just stand there silently, and guess what? You are probably going to do that anyway.

All right. Here goes nothing.

Opening the door, I see the bar packed with people. I exhale deeply and squeeze my way in from the outside. As I pass by body after body, a hand reaches out and wraps around my waist.

McGruff?

No. Not McGruff. Definitely not McGruff.

I look up at a sweaty guy peering creepily down at me.

"Hey there, sugar."

"Sorry, I'm just passing by."

I push his hand off my hip.

"Whoa. Don't go. Dance with me."

"There's no music."

"Hey, don't be like that."

He grabs my arm.

"Please, let me leave."

"Hey!"

Before I realize what is happening, McGruff is pushing the guy back and yelling at him.

"Back off!"

"Sorry, man. I didn't know she was yours. Calm down."

"I will not calm down."

McGruff pushes him again, and his friends rush over to stop him.

"Hey, Nate. Cool down," John says.

The crowd around us pushes back and forms a circle around us. I can see the bartender staring at us. Another man comes out from behind the bar and walks in our direction. McGruff's friends drag him out of the bar before we all get kicked out.

"Hands off!" McGruff yells as we all spill out of the bar.

"Look, Nate, we're just trying to help," George says.

"You were going to get into a fight with that guy and his friends," Pete says.

"The owner was about to kick us out," Dan adds.

"Are you okay, Nate?" John asks.

McGruff had walked about ten paces up the street and just turned around to start walking back.

"I'm fine. You can all go. I'm not going back in there."

Does that include me? Can I go now? Am I dismissed?

Seems like a legitimate question.

"Are you sure?" John asks.

"Yes. I'm fine. I will talk to you all later."

That includes me, right? I'm part of the all?

The four of them kibitz for a second and then cross the street and walk into Flannery's.

Bastards. They didn't even invite me.

Why would they?

Shut up.

You clearly weren't included in the all that McGruff was talking about.

This is bullshit. What am I supposed to do?

Well, you can talk to McGruff.

How about I call a Road Trip?

No. Talk to McGruff.

His hands on his hips, he's looking down at the sidewalk. We are only three feet apart and are the only ones on the sidewalk at the moment, but neither of us have broken the silence.

Say something.

Say what?

Anything.

Nope.

Say words, Gemma. Say words.

That guy deserved it?

No. Not those words.

Should we go to Flannery's?

No! Not those words, either.

You look really mad.

Nope. None of those words.

We good?

God damn it, Gemma.

"You have nothing to say?" McGruff finally breaks the silence.

I think that is apparent.

"What do you want me to say?" I ask.

"Oh, I don't know. That you're sorry?"

"Sorry? For what?"

"You've been in a bad mood for weeks. And then that guy…"

"What? Like I had anything to do with that guy. He was a jerk."

"Yeah and I had to go and save you, and I got into a fight at my bar."

"Save me? You didn't have to start the fight. I could've just walked away."

"Oh, that's right. You won't let me save you. Only Nick can save you."

"What does that mean?"

"You're constantly pushing me away, and yet you gush about how Nick is your savior."

"First of all, I don't gush about Nick. And he's not my savior."

"Ugh. I never would have gotten into a bar fight before I met you. This isn't me."

"I didn't know that. How was I supposed to know that about you?"

"You would have if you didn't keep running away from me."

"I can't help that!"

"And I can't help that I don't feel like I'm in control when I'm around you. Before I met you, I was always in control. I even was when I first started talking to you. I had my life all under control."

"Is that why you liked me? Because you thought I'd be easy to control? Because I'm so skittish? Well, joke's on you because I am never in control. *I* can't even control me. So, you can't either. You're just going to have to live with it. So, sucks to be both of us!"

"That's not what I meant! I meant that I'm not in control of me. And it's all because of you."

"Ugh! I can't even talk to you right now. I don't want to see you, either," I say.

"They're sending me on a business trip, so you don't have to see me. So there."

I turn around away from him and pull my phone out of my purse.

"Are you calling a Road Trip?"

"Yes," I answer flatly.

"Why?"

"Because I don't want to be here anymore."

"That's right. Just run away like you usually do, after you started the fight."

"Me? None of this is my fault!"

"What do you want me to do?"

"Go back inside so I don't have to see you anymore," I reply.

"Fine."

Immediately turning, he throws open the door and disappears inside.

Don't cry. Don't you dare cry. This is not your fault. Sure, you've been cranky lately, but that's no reason to yell at you like that. This is not your fault.

My lip starts to quiver, and my hands shake. My Road Trip will be here in four minutes. I can make it until then without crying. I know I can.

You will be fine. You will be fine.

Just then, the guy that grabbed me earlier, stumbles out of the bar and careens towards me.

Shit! Shit! Shit!

"Hey there," he drolls. "Where is your boyfriend? He just leave you here alone?"

As a matter of fact, yes he did. That bastard.

I just awkwardly smile and take a few steps away from him. I look down at my phone. Two minutes until Johnny shows up in his Hyundai.

You can do this. Just ignore him. He's just a drunken asshole.

"Don't be rude. I hate when girls ignore me when I am talking right to them. Or maybe you're just a dumb bitch that can't hold a conversation. Is that it?"

Do not lose your mind, Gemma. Do not lose your mind. You will be fine. Just breathe. Just breathe.

"Just give me a smile. Just one smile, and I will leave you alone."

No! Don't you dare smile at that bastard. Don't you dare.

"Oh, come on! Don't be a bitch."

He steps closer to me, and I counter by stepping back.

"You're such a bitch! I should have known from the bar."

He moves closer to me as a Hyundai pulls up a few steps down the street. Trying to avoid him and put the car in between us, I walk into the street and get into the car from the driver's side. Slamming the door, I let out a huge breath.

Breathe. Just breathe.

But I don't. The guy opens the passenger side door and peers in.

"You just gonna leave like that, you bitch? I ought to..."

Before he finishes his sentence, I see him violently fall onto the pavement. McGruff gets into the car next to me and slams the door shut before the guy can even react.

I glare at him from across the seat.

"Everything okay back there? Is this okay?" the driver tentatively asks.

McGruff just stares back at me.

"Yes," I say. "It's okay. Please drive."

"You got it," the driver says and peels away from the curb as the drunk guy gets to his feet. We can hear him yelling profanities as we drive away.

Still looking at McGruff, I turn my head and look out the window. My heart is still pounding.

Breathe, Gemma. Calm down. You're fine. Just breathe.

The driver doesn't say a word, and I am thankful. I can barely keep myself from crying.

It's okay. Don't cry. Don't you dare cry. You are almost home. You are fine.

Gem of Uncertainty

My right hand is resting on the seat next to me. I feel McGruff slowly move his hand over mine and circle his fingers around my palm. I don't move my hand. But I don't look at him, either.

Don't you dare cry.

What is it about the smallest gesture of caring during an emotional time that makes me want to cry even more?

Don't you dare.

The car pulls up in front of my apartment building.

Should I say something? Should I even look at him?

No. Just get out.

I open the door and step out with my left foot, but McGruff doesn't let go of my hand.

Bastard.

I tug, but he doesn't relent. Sighing, I turn to look at him. His eyes are large and watery and he has a look of... What is that? Desperation? Vulnerability?

Without saying anything, I pull my hand from his, get out of the car, and slam the door.

CHAPTER FIVE

Nope. Nope. Nope. This can't be happening. Why is it time already? Can't I just cancel this meeting? No one will ever know.

Who are you kidding? Jack will absolutely tell Carl that you canceled on him. There is no way he won't.

Why couldn't I have set up one meeting with both Jack and Nick? Then I wouldn't have to be alone with Jack.

Because Carl told you that you couldn't.

Oh, God. There he goes. He just walked past my desk to go to the conference room. Damn it. He's on time. Why couldn't he be ten minutes late like he always is, so I don't have to spend as much time with him?

Because life is not fair.

Don't I know it.

Gemma, you have to get up. You have to go to the meeting. He's already in there.

No, I don't. Do I? What if I just don't go?

He will come looking for you. He has to walk right by your desk to get back to his own. He will find you.

Damn it all to hell.

I take a deep breath and release it slowly. I can do this.

Just don't be an idiot.

Not helping!

Locking my computer screen, I grab my pen and pad of paper and stand up.

You can definitely do this.

There is no chance that I can do this.

I slowly walk down the aisle and into the conference room and close the door behind me.

Gem of Uncertainty

You have to sit directly across from him; otherwise, this meeting will be weird, and he will definitely let you know that.

It will be weird no matter what.

"You're late," he says as I sit down across from him.

For the love of all things holy, like this man can even talk. He is constantly speed walking down the halls to get to meetings that have already started.

I force a smile.

"Okay," I say. "I only have a few…"

"I wanted to start with these," he says, interrupting me and pointing to a piece of paper in front of him.

Of course, he does. Why did I think that I would be able to run this meeting when it will clearly be run by him? And it will undoubtedly go off the rails within ten minutes, probably less.

"So, you need to change this requirement for this homeowner's coverage. It won't convert correctly," he says.

"Okay."

That wasn't that bad.

You just jinxed it.

And I did. He starts his monologue with other requirements that need to be changed and then quickly goes off on a rant about how the go-live went and how he has too much to do to be sitting in a requirements meeting with me.

Same to you, bud. I don't have the time or the will power to be sitting here alone in a room with you.

"It's just that I have to start programming the new states, and no one understands how much work it is because no one helps me. They just dumped it all on me and expect it to get done on time and accurately. It's not right. I need help," he says.

Yes. Yes, he does.

My heartbeat has reached a sprint, and my ears begin to ring. My head starts to spin.

Calm down, Gemma. Calm down. It's just stupid Jack. Just let him rant, and you will be fine.

"That's why I need this changed."

Shit. Need what changed?

Gemma, you need to listen. Listen. No one is here to take notes for you. You have to ask him what you missed. You have to ask him.

No. I can't. I can't even look at him.

You have to; otherwise, he will call you out in front of everyone. You know he will.

Without lifting my eyes from my paper, I ask, "What was it that you needed changed, again?"

"Ugh! It was the tax field on the vehicle page. Don't you ever listen? I said it clearly."

No. I don't listen. Obviously.

I scribble down my notes without responding or looking at him.

Just breathe. This has to be almost over. Just breathe.

"Gemma, did you get that?"

I physically flinch.

Shit. Why did I do that? He thinks I am even more idiotic than he already does.

That's probably not even possible.

"Well, did you?" he barks.

My heart is about to pound out of my chest. My breathing is shallow, and my head feels like it's floating.

"Yes," I say quietly.

"Are you sure? What did I say?"

For the love of goodness, can this meeting be over now? I can hardly breathe. I can't even look up from my paper.

"You said the tax field on the vehicle page."

"Well, wonders never cease," he says.

Does he have to be so mean?

"I'll tell you something. I have never been on a project like this in all my career. I have to do all of this myself and the timeline is never pushed back for any reason and that is not right at all. I say..."

But he doesn't get to say anything else. Nick barges through the door.

"Oh, sorry," Nick says. "I thought I was late. Is this over?"

He looks at Jack, and then his amused eyes look at me.

"I guess it is now," Jack says, roughly gets up from his seat, and walks past Nick and out the door. Nick closes it behind him.

I let out a huge sigh, put my elbows on the table, and run my hands over my head and through my hair.

"Thank you so much," I say. "I don't think I could have lasted one more second."

"Just doing what I was told."

"And I whole-heartedly appreciate that."

Nick sits directly opposite me, where Jack had just been sitting.

"Ew, still warm," he says and cringes.

"Gross." I laugh at his expression, and my shoulders drop. My heartbeat starts to slow down, and I can feel my whole body relax.

You did it. Good job. You made it through the entire meeting without crying, yelling, or getting up and storming off. Great job.

I flinched. He saw. It was not a great job.

Stop being so hard on yourself. That was a hell storm of a meeting, and you are still alive. And Jack is still alive. That was a success.

It was just the first meeting.

Stop it. Think positively. What happened to all that positive self-talk Stacey told you about?

It's okay to not be perfect.

There you go. You can do this.

"Gemma?"

Oh, hey, yeah I'm still in a meeting with Nick. I should really be present for meetings if there are only two of us in it. I need to work on that.

Yes, you should. Like right now. Gemma!

"Yeah, sorry," I say. "It's been a weird few days. I'm kind of out of it."

"I get it," he says. "You're still on an emotional high from P2 going live and the Fenway party."

I wish.

"Or maybe," he continues, "you're on an emotional low because of the start of P3. I get that, too. Oh, wait. It's an emotional rollercoaster of back and forth between the two."

He's not wrong. Not completely, anyway.

"I wish that's all it was."

"Care to talk about it?"

Do I? Maybe. But with Nick?

What's wrong with Nick?

Nothing. But he's a coworker.

You mean your work husband?

Shut up. He's not. Obviously. I just feel weird talking to a coworker about my dating life.

You talk to Brittany.

She's different. She's a friend.

And a coworker.

"You don't have to if you don't want to," Nick says to my silence. "I didn't mean to pry."

"No. It's okay. I just got into a fight with someone this weekend."

Someone? That's vague.

"Ah, the illusive someone."

See, even Nick thought it was weird wording.

"The guy I've been seeing."

"Oh, McGruff."

Ugh. I wish Brittany hadn't told him that nickname.

"Yes. Him."

"Was it a bad fight?"

75

Was it? It was our first fight. He did get pretty mad at me, and I'm still not entirely sure why.

You should talk to someone about it.

Like who? Nick?

How about Stacey? You do remember your therapist, don't you? The one you canceled on for two weeks in a row.

McGruff did apologize. He sent me a text immediately. And the next day and the day after that. He does seem sorry. But there is something else. I am not sure what exactly. For some reason, I still don't want to talk to him.

"It was sort of bad."

Nice. Still vague.

"I see," he says.

"Yeah, let's not talk about this."

"Right. Yeah. I'm sorry I brought it up."

"No, it's okay. Don't worry about it."

"I did have a great time at Fenway, though. It was probably the most fun I've had at a work party before," he says.

"Me too! I had so much fun. I was surprised. I really liked hanging out with you and Brittany."

"You were surprised that you had fun with me and Brittany?"

"That's not what I meant. And you know it."

"I know." Nick smiles. "I had a surprising amount of fun, as well. Who knew Fred was such a dancer?"

"Oh, my God! I would never come back to work if I danced at a work party. He must have been so drunk."

"Indeed. Free booze can do that to you."

"When Barb started dancing with him, I thought I was going to lose it."

Nick laughs out loud. "I know! The look on Bob's face was priceless. He was like, 'I can't believe I hired these weirdos.'"

Now I laugh out loud. "Oh, my God. And Carl trying to stop them. I almost died."

"He was like, 'Excuse me, can you please stop this madness? You are embarrassing me in front of the Pesky Pole.'"

"I can't believe they both came back to work after that. You would never see me again."

"Oh, come on. I would see you."

There's something in the way he says it that makes me stop and stare at him. He is so serious, like it's obvious that we would still see each other.

Why am I still staring at him? He is staring back. Look down. Look down.

I drop my eyes to the table.

For the love of goodness, Gemma. What was that? That was a moment. That was definitely a moment.

No, it wasn't. It's just Nick.

The way he looked at you.

Shut up.

There is a knock on the door, and my head spins around to see Carl peeking into the room.

"Hey, guys, wrap it up. You're over time," he says and gently closes the door, again.

What? I look at my watch. We are two minutes over time. How did that happen? I look up at Nick, who is still staring at me.

"I guess we need to go," I say. "Sorry, we didn't get anything done."

"It's okay. I liked this better," he says, his eyes looking softly into mine.

Get up and run away. Get up and run away, now.

And I do. I get up and quickly walk to the door. I can see Carl's legs waiting outside the room.

"Hey, Gemma?" Nick says.

I turn, a step before the door, still closed, and look at Nick, still standing at the opposite end of the table. He hasn't moved at all, and he has this weird look in his eyes that I haven't seen before. What is that?

"Yeah?"

What the hell is happening? He doesn't say anything, but he keeps opening his mouth slightly and then closing it. He has big puppy dog eyes.

What is this?

Is he going to kiss you?

No!

Are you sure?

Yes. It's Nick. And besides, he is across the room. It's physically impossible.

He can run.

Shut up. That's not what this is.

Then what is this?

I have no idea.

He still hasn't said anything. I tilt my head to the side and furrow my brow.

Say something.

No.

You can't just stand here and stare at each other all day.

We can't?

No. Carl has booked the room after you. He is waiting.

Really? That's the only reason we can't just stand here and stare at each other all day?

Then say something.

No.

This is weird, Gemma.

I don't know if I want to hear what he has to say. Look at him. He is breathing deeply, and his hands are shaking. He's looking at me with such...what is that?

Passion.

Shut up!

It is. You can't tell me it's not. For the love of God, say something, Gemma. This is getting super weird.

Say what?

Literally anything.

"Nick..."

"Gemma..."

What the?

I straighten up and look back at his big watery eyes as he takes a tentative step toward me.

Nope. Make him stop. Step back. Do something. Damn it, Gemma. Do something!

But I don't. I don't do anything. I just stand there dumbfounded as he keeps taking step after hesitant step until he is standing a foot away from me.

"Gemma..."

His hand moves slightly.

Holy crap. Is he going to touch your hand? Stop this, Gemma. Stop this madness! What the hell is happening? Make it stop. Say something.

But I don't. He continues to stare softly into my eyes.

"Gemma..."

His hand moves again.

Stop this!

But I don't. As he slowly reaches for my hand, his fingers slightly touch the back of my hand.

My heart is pounding. When did my heart start pounding?

You need to stop this. Think of McGruff. What is Nick doing?

His fingers softly move across the skin on the back of my hand. He is still staring into my eyes when the fire alarm blasts out, and the sprinklers in the conference room open at full blast.

As Carl opens the door to the room, I turn to look at him. Nick drops his hand, and I let out a huge breath.

"You two need to get out of here. We need to evacuate!"

Awkwardly, I move toward the door. I take two steps out of the room and stop. Everyone is walking towards the exits, but the sprinklers aren't on. No one else is soaked. Nick stops next to me.

"Just us getting drenched then?" he asks.

I shrug and wipe a drop of water from my forehead. "Guess so."

We just look at each other for a moment before we both start laughing.

"Guys! Move!" Carl yells at us.

"Geesh," Nick says. "He is not even concerned that we are dripping." He rolls his eyes. "Let's go."

We follow the crowd to the doors and slowly, starting and stopping, as people dump in from other floors, we walk down twenty-two flights of stairs.

And I thought the slit of death was bad. This is way worse. And I'm in heels.

Nick starts out next to me, but in the crowd on the stairs, he drops back behind a few people as they barge into the stairwell from the exit doors.

You know, this isn't so bad. You get to walk down in silence with no one talking to you. Sure, it's twenty-two flights of stairs, but at least wherever the fire is, it's not near you.

Jeepers. Thanks for bringing that up.

I take a deep breath and continue my silent, even though there's noise all around me, journey down to the ground. Everyone in the building empties out onto Federal Street. The street is effectively blocked off from traffic, despite the fire marshals trying to herd everyone onto the sidewalks. The fire alarm can be heard through the door as people are still coming out.

It's a few minutes before the fire trucks arrive. The crowd parts for them, and the firemen enter the building.

"Gemma."

My head spins to the left. McGruff is standing next to me.

"I was looking all over for you," he says. McGruff places his palm on my cheek. "Why are you so soaked?"

"Just lucky, I guess."

His thumb slowly wipes the water dripping down my face.

"Still mad at me?"

"You can't control me."

"Oh, don't I know it."

He drops his hand from my face and takes my hand in his.

"I think it's a real fire," he says.

"The sprinklers in the conference room I was in really thought so, too."

We all wait for what feels to be about twenty minutes before word spreads that the HVAC unit caught fire and is no longer functioning. Because it is almost ninety degrees today, they are sending us all home. A few minutes later, I receive a text from Carl to his entire department saying the same thing.

McGruff puts his own phone back into his pocket.

"I guess they are letting us all go home," he says.

"Same here."

"We've been out here for a while. You didn't complain about the heat at all," McGruff says.

"Yeah, well I am soaked."

McGruff awkwardly smiles. "Let me walk you home."

"No. I'm okay. I just need to change."

"You sure?"

"Yep."

He awkwardly smiles, again. "I will talk to you tomorrow, then?"

"Sure."

I let my hand drop from his, slowly take a few steps backward, and turn to walk away from him.

Damn it. You should have let him walk you home. He clearly isn't still mad at you.

Well, maybe I am mad at him. Does he really want to control me? Is that the only reason he likes me? Because he is in control? What else is there kicking around in the back of my mind? Why do I still want to avoid him?

Sons of bitches.

The next morning, my laptop connects to my work computer without an issue.

They couldn't have given us one measly day off? Not one? They have to get the computers up and running the very next day?

Pulling up my email, I read the most recent message in my inbox. It is from the CEO. We are to remain working from home for the remainder of the week. The building management company has scheduled the HVAC company to replace the unit on the roof on Monday. We will resume normal business hours on Tuesday of next week. Until then, keep up business as usual as much as possible from home.

One week working from home. It's like a dream come true. I don't have to see anyone. I don't have to get hip checked into the wall by Barb. I don't have to see Jack. I don't have to see Nick.

You just put Nick in the same bucket as Barb and Jack? What is up with that?

There was that weird moment in the conference room.

It was probably nothing. You probably just read way too much into it. You probably just imagined it.

Probably. But to be safe, and since we are working from home, I bring up my calendar and cancel all of the meetings I have booked for the rest of the week, including the meetings I have with Nick and Jack scheduled for this week and Monday of next week.

There is such a thing as virtual meetings, you know?

No. This is a week off from all that. I am canceling them, and that is the end of the story. I get a week of peace. I don't have to see anyone. Literally.

Including McGruff?

Yes, including McGruff. Especially McGruff. I don't have to see his perfect face waiting for me outside of Sally's or after work. I don't have to see his face at all because I am not leaving my apartment all week. That's right. I don't have to. Imagine that.

Don't get too excited. It's only a week.

A glorious week.

Speaking of, is this the spot you are choosing to work? Sitting at your breakfast bar? This is so uncomfortable.

Where else should I go? It's not like I have a home office or even a desk. Space is limited here. I can work on the couch and the coffee table. I can try that for a while.

Picking up my laptop, I walk over to the couch, sit, and put my computer on the coffee table in front of me. This is much more comfortable, but not at all conducive to working. What am I supposed to do, sit hunched over all day? I peek over at my bed.

No. No. The couch is good enough. No need to get greedy here. You are home for a week. Let's act professional. You need to keep up your work and not slack off; otherwise, Carl will find out. It's only a week. Try to keep your regular schedule, get up at the same time every day. This will be over soon. Don't get used to it.

And why are you wearing normal clothes? Look at you. You are wearing jeans and a nice shirt. No one can see you. Why are you dressed?

Note to self: wear leggings and a T-shirt tomorrow. I have to take advantage of working from home while I can.

Speaking of, all of your meetings are canceled. Look at your inbox. Everyone else canceled their meetings, too.

Holy moly! A week at home and no meetings? This is the best week ever! I will have no stress.

My phone buzzes. It's McGruff.

I sigh. So much for no stress.

"How is working from home today?" he asks.

"It's fine," I reply.

Goodness, Gemma. Be a little friendlier, would you?

I don't want to. There is something...

What?

He made me feel...

He made you feel what?

He made me feel bad about my anxiety. He made me self-conscious about how I run away from him and push him away. That's it. That's the other reason I've been missing. He made me feel like there is something wrong with me, that my anxiety is a problem. I felt like he was attacking me on a personal level. It's not just that he wanted to control me, but that he didn't understand, or wouldn't understand, my anxiety and how it makes me react. He doesn't understand me.

"Do you still want to go out on Friday?" he texts again.

"No," I reply. "I need to get some stuff done around my apartment."

Liar.

"Okay," he responds.

You lied.

I did. But I don't want to feel like this around the person I am dating. No one should make me feel like this, especially him.

What are you going to do about it?

Just cancel our Friday plans, for now.

CHAPTER SIX

Here I am, sitting in the waiting room, picking at my cuticles, awaiting my exciting Friday night plans.

Hey, you chose seeing your therapist over seeing McGruff. You should have canceled like you wanted to and just lain on the couch all night.

I couldn't cancel again. That would have been three weeks in a row. That's a bit much. Besides, it's too late now. I am here.

It's not too late. She hasn't seen you yet. You're the only one here in the waiting room, so you can just quietly sneak out.

I can't do that. She will still charge me for the appointment even though I didn't see her.

It would be worth it. You could go home, get into your pajamas, and lie on the couch like Friday nights are supposed to be spent.

I guess I could. I have already canceled on McGruff.

Yes! Get up and leave. She will just make you talk about your feelings. That's gross. You don't want to do that. And she will force you to talk about McGruff. You don't want to do that, either. Stand up. Let's go.

"Gemma?"

Shit. It's too late. She's seen you. You took too long to decide. You should have cut and run when you had the chance.

"Are you coming?" she inquires.

"Oh, yeah."

Duh.

Standing up, I follow her down the hallway of closed doors and into a room on the right. I sit in the chair on the opposite side of the room and place my purse onto the seat next to me.

Stacy is probably in her forties, maybe five feet two inches tall, if that, with a slender frame. Her blonde hair is still in a pixie haircut. As she closes the door, her blue eyes look into mine.

"I haven't seen you for a while," she says as she sits, crosses her legs, and picks up a pen and a pad of paper.

Shit. I knew this was a bad idea. I should have gone home and put on my pajamas.

See. Told you.

Shut up.

I don't answer Stacey. I just shrug.

"Tell me how you've been."

"I've been okay."

She nods and waits for more.

Well, this is going well. You have to talk, Gemma. That's the whole point of coming here. She is expecting you to talk. Look at her. She is waiting. Say something, Gemma. Say anything.

But, I don't.

"Okay. Let's start with your medication. The last we talked, Janet had just upped your dosage. How have you been feeling?"

Damn it. You should have picked the topic. Now she is asking about your feelings.

What should I tell her? I don't know how I've been feeling. It's been a weird few weeks.

Tell her that.

"Honestly, I'm not sure. I've been tired, and I don't feel like doing anything. I've canceled on you and Liz a couple of times. And Nate, too. I canceled on him tonight."

"Because you didn't feel like going out at all?"

"Partly. And partly because we haven't been getting along all that great. I think a lot of it is my fault. I've been acting off, and I don't know how to fix it."

"How have you been acting?"

"I get mad, and I snap at both Liz and Nate for no good reason."

"So, you've been more irritable."

"Yes."

"And you think you've lost your motivation to do some things as well?"

"Yes. I hardly ever want to go out. It's like it's a chore, and my friends have to beg me to go out. I just have no motivation, and I'm also really tired all the time. But, I guess once I do go out, it's not so bad."

"You've been tired, as well? Have you had any trouble sleeping?"

"I always do."

"How is your anxiety? Is it getting better?"

"Honestly, no. I don't think it's better at all."

"When is your next appointment with Janet?"

"Next week."

"Okay. I suspect that you've been having some unwanted side effects from the Zoloft. SSRIs can cause fatigue, loss of motivation, and even irritability. That would explain why you don't feel like yourself."

Holy crap. So, it's not me. There is an explanation for me acting so poorly to everyone. I am not purposefully sabotaging my time with McGruff or intentionally canceling on Liz. I'm not a complete asshole.

"Gemma?"

"Honestly, that makes me feel a lot better. I thought I was going crazy. I didn't feel like myself, but I had no idea why."

"I'm glad. I wouldn't be surprised if she switched your medication. But don't stop taking it or change your dose until you see her again."

"A new medication? I have to start this all over, again? What if I react the same way on that one?"

Stacey sighs. "I know. It's a process, but there are no short cuts. Unfortunately, it's trial and error. No person reacts the same to medications as another person. You just have to try them and see which is right for you."

"Oh."

"I know it's hard, Gemma. But you are on the right track. Don't give up now. You will feel better. I promise."

"Okay."

"You just have to promise me that you will not cancel on Janet, and you will keep your appointment next week."

Damn it all to hell.

"Okay."

She makes one of those awkward half smiles and half frowns.

"To improve your mood, do you exercise at all?"

Son of a bitch. I knew this would come up eventually.

"Not really."

"Well, studies have shown that exercise can improve someone's mood. Maybe try some light jogging?"

Jogging? Is she for real?

"Okay," she continues, presumably as a reaction to my face. "Maybe just some walking."

"I walk to the Common a lot. But not when it is hot out."

"That is good. Keep that up."

I sigh.

"Okay."

Damn it. She told me to exercise. When has exercise ever made someone feel better?

She did say there were studies.

Shut up!

"Tell me about what has happened with Nate. You said you haven't been getting along lately?"

Oh, here we go.

"Yeah. We had a fight last weekend. I barely talked to him this week, and I canceled on him tonight."

"Why did you cancel?"

"Well, partly because I am just so tired now. And partly because I am still mad at him. I was really irritable the last couple of times I've seen him, and I snapped at him a few times. And this past weekend, we ended up yelling at each other outside of the bar we were at."

"Yelling about what?"

"The fact that he can't control me."

"Control you? In what way?"

"Not in a bad way. He's never been controlling in any way. He just had complete control over how we met and how our relationship played out. I was worried that he only wanted to date me because he could control me and the situation."

"Did you tell him that?"

"I sort of yelled it at him."

"And what did he say?"

"That it wasn't true. He just needs to feel like he is in control and when he's around me, he doesn't feel that way."

"Do you know why he needs to feel in control?"

"No, we stopped talking to each other, and I've kind of been ignoring him all week."

"Okay. Well, may I suggest that you ask him why he feels the need to be in control? And, also, why he feels so out of control around you? Can you do that?"

Say no. Don't do that. Say no.

"Yes, I probably can."

"Good."

That was not a no.

Shut up. This will be good for me. For both me and McGruff.

"I won't be able to soon, though. He is going on a business trip."

"And you don't plan on talking to him at all while he's gone?"

Nope.

You should really talk to him. Plus, you have a full week before he leaves.

"I guess I will."

"Good. Is there anything else on your mind that you'd like to talk about?"

Tell her about Nick. My goodness, tell her about Nick.

What would I even say about him?

That he practically kissed you at work in the conference room.

He didn't, though. I am sure I imagined that.

"I think my boss is going to make me rejoin the daily meeting soon."

What was that? That's not about Nick.

"Oh no. How are you feeling about it?"

Shitty McShit Shit. That's how I am feeling.

"Not good."

"I can imagine."

"These last few weeks have been great. I mean, not great, but better than they were. I don't have to deal with all of the yelling and arguing that goes on in there."

"It must have been nice."

"It was. And now it's over."

"Maybe. But you survived before, and you will survive again. And it's not forever, right? It's just until the end of the project."

"Yes, and this is the final phase."

"Well, that's something."

I sigh and look down at my bloody cuticles.

"What is it, Gemma?"

"I just can't stop thinking about Nate wanting to control me. And it's not even that. I'm not sure he understands my anxiety. He made me self-conscious about it the other night when he said I was always running away from him. I don't think he understands me or could ever understand me."

"Do you know the cause of controlling behavior?"

"No."

"Well, it's not the same in every case, but some of the time, it is caused by underlying anxiety. The need to be in control is how they deal with uncertainty and anxiety."

Anxiety? McGruff?

"Really? He doesn't seem anxious."

"Not all people with anxiety exhibit the same behavior."

"I don't know."

"It can't hurt to talk about it. You may have more in common with Nate than you think."

I don't buy it.

"Have you talked to him about your anxiety?" she asks.

"He knows I have it."

"I mean, how you feel, and why you feel it?"

"No, I haven't."

"Have you talked to him about the medication you are taking?"

"No."

"Why not?"

"I don't know."

"Are you embarrassed by it?"

Embarrassed? Yeah, probably.

"Maybe."

"There is no reason to be. It is not your fault."

"I know."

"It may help him understand you more if he knows what you are going through with your anxiety and the side effects of your medication."

Talk to McGruff about it? Really?

"You seem hesitant."

"I guess I am."

"Why?"

"I don't want him to know."

"To know about what?"

"I don't know."

"There is nothing to be embarrassed about. You should be able to talk to your partner about these things."

Partner? Are we partners? What are we?

Stacey narrows her eyes.

"You reacted to the word partner."

Damn. She's so observant.

"Do you not consider yourself partners? What do you consider you and Nate to be?" she asks.

"I'm not sure."

"Maybe that's part of the problem. You aren't sure of what you two are, so you don't want to confide in him."

"That could be it."

"Do you not want to be in a relationship with him?"

"Yes, I do. It's just…"

"It's just what?"

"Now I don't know if he likes me or just likes that I can be controlled."

"I think we've established that you can't be controlled."

I smile. "I guess so."

"So, what is it then? Do you know what he thinks you two are?"

"No."

"Maybe that's something else you should talk about."

"Maybe."

Damn. I hate when Stacey gives me homework. Therapy homework is so much worse than school homework. Why do I have to do so much sharing, talking, and soul searching? Does everyone else have to do this? Does everyone else get so much homework at therapy?

Well, you need to do it. You need to talk to McGruff about so much.

Shut up.

"Are you seeing Liz tomorrow night?"

"I'm not sure."

"I think you should. Not only to get out of your apartment, but to talk to someone besides me."

Talking to myself doesn't count?

Absolutely not.

But my apartment is so cool and comfortable, and outside is so hot and uncomfortable.

"Gemma?"

"Okay. I will see her."

Damn that Stacey. I should have just told Liz that I would stay in tonight. I would be on the couch with my face tucked cozily into a pillow instead of sitting in the backseat of this smelly sedan listening to reggae music.

Calm down, Gemma. Your heart is starting to pound. There is no need to be so upset. These are your usual Saturday night plans. You will feel better when you see Liz.

Now, I'm not even sure if I am really upset or if it's the medication making me upset. Life was so much less complicated when I could just blame everything on myself and my inescapable anxiety. The universe had to go and throw a monkey wrench right into the middle of my usual neuroses so I don't even know what I am feeling anymore and if what I am feeling is actually real or a symptom of the medication I am taking to make myself feel better, which is inexplicably making me feel worse.

The driver lets me out in front of Flannery's. I walk through the door, over to Liz, pull out the seat next to her, and sit down. Before I even order, Greg sets down my drink in front of me, winks at me, and walks away.

"Hey," Liz says.

"Hey, how is everything?"

"Fine. You?"

"Fine."

"Did you see Nate last night?"

Damn. Straight to business.

"No. I canceled on him."

"Did you see him today?"

"No."

"Will you see him tomorrow?"

"No."

"Did you talk to him at all during the week?"

"No."

"Why not?"

"I'm not sure I am over our fight."

"Do you honestly think he wants to control you?"

"I don't know."

"Gem, we all know you are uncontrollable. He knew that from the beginning when you ran out of here when he came to say hi."

"Then why did he say that he wants to control me?"

"I don't know. Is that it, though? That's why you don't want to see him? Because you think he wants to control you?"

"No. I just don't think he understands me."

"You have barely given him a chance."

We both look out the window in the direction of O'Brady's.

"Do you think he's over there?" Liz asks.

"Probably."

"Do you think he'll come over?"

"I doubt it."

"Do you want to go over there?"

"No!"

"Are you sure?"

"Yes, that would be weird."

"It's not weird. You would be going to say hi to your boyfriend. Plus, he stalked you for weeks. You can go see him once."

Boyfriend?

"I don't want to."

"No? Let's just go over and see if he's there. We don't have to go in."

"Do what? Look in the windows?"

"Yes."

"Like a couple of creeps?"

"Yes."

"Liz."

"What?"

"What's the point?"

"To see him."

"From afar?"

"Yes."

"That's weird."

"So? We will see if he's there and then decide if we want to go in or not."

"It is strange to go over and stare in the window."

"Okay, that's not a no," Liz says. "Greg, we will be back."

"Can I come?" Greg asks.

"No," Liz says.

"Sure," I say.

"No," Liz says and turns to glare pointedly at me.

"We'll be back," I say.

"Fine." Greg pouts.

As I follow Liz out onto the sidewalk, Barry passes by and goes into the pub.

"Hi, ladies," he says as the door closes.

"You should have let Greg come," I say.

Liz rolls her eyes.

Traffic is light, so we walk briskly across Boylston Street and stop in front of the door to O'Brady's. I can hear the roar of conversations as a man opens the door, leaves the bar, and walks down the street.

I look at Liz. "Now what?"

"Do you want to go in?"

"No."

"So, we creepily look in the window, then?"

"I guess."

Liz and I take a few steps to the right and position ourselves next to, but not in front of, the window.

"Can you see him?" I ask.

"No. Can you?"

"No. Oh, wait. I think that might be John."

"Where?"

"Over by the right side of the bar."

"Yeah. I think that's him. Do you see Nate?"

"Not yet."

"Hey, you two!"

I physically jump and turn to see McGruff standing next to us.

"What are you doing?" he asks.

"What are we doing? What are you doing?" I ask.

Oh, my God, Gemma. Really? What is he doing? He is clearly doing what he does every Saturday night.

"Well, I am meeting my friends like I usually do."

"You're late," I say.

"Yes, I am. I wasn't sure I was going to go out after last week," he says. "How are you, Liz?"

"Oh, I'm good, thanks."

He nods. "So, what brings you two across the street?"

"Nothing," I say.

"Nothing?" he asks.

"Nope."

And before he or Liz can respond, I spin around and speed walk across the street.

Damn it, Gemma. That was so stupid. He clearly knows you were there to see him. You could have at least stayed and talked to him.

And say what? Yes, I'm stalking you.

96

For a start, yes. You clearly wanted to see him; otherwise, you wouldn't have let Liz talk you into going over there.

Doesn't matter. I ran away, per the usual. I am sure McGruff will be mad about it. According to him, I am always running away from him. I just hope Liz doesn't feel too awkward.

I am sure she is used to it. You've left her in far more awkward situations than this one. And according to *everyone*, you are always running away from him. This is not subjective. You are actually *always* running away from him. You literally just did.

Okay. Okay. I get it. He has a point.

I walk back into Flannery's and reclaim my seat at the bar. Our drinks haven't been touched. I pick up mine and take a couple of large swigs.

"How'd that go?" Greg asks.

"Not good, Greg. Not good."

He smiles and waits for Liz to walk through the door and sit back down next to me.

"Mission accomplished?" he asks her.

"Not quite."

He smirks and walks away.

"I'm sorry. I had to leave. Was Nate mad?"

"No. He was actually kind of glad that you came by to stalk him. He was under the impression that you were pretty mad at him. He didn't know if you wanted to see him, so he was glad to see that you did. I think he was kind of happy that you were following him around for once."

"Oh."

Barry stands behind our chairs and in between us. I can feel him hovering, so I turn around.

"Would you ladies like to play darts?"

Liz looks at me.

"No," I say. "But you go."

"No, not if you aren't. Sorry, Barry. Not tonight."

"Okay," Barry mumbles and walks away.

"You disappointed Barry," Liz says.

"I am constantly disappointing Barry," I say. "He is used to it."

"True. Anything else new in your life?"

"Well, I am still working from home. They are apparently fixing the HVAC unit on Monday, so we will be back in the office on Tuesday morning."

"Oh, that stinks you have to go back to the office so soon."

"I know."

"How has it been working from home?"

"It's been glorious. Everyone canceled their meetings, like we all unconsciously and unanimously decided that this week would be meeting free because we aren't in the office. I didn't have to meet with Jack. Or Nick."

"But you like Nick, right?"

"Right."

Right? Why haven't you told her about the weirdness between you two.

"Yeah, I can see how working from home would be nice. One more day of it."

"Yeah, I am going to miss it."

My phone buzzes, and I look down. It's a text from McGruff.

"It was nice to see you, even if you did run away. I really don't mind. I will always catch you."

See. Maybe he would understand.

"Why are you blushing?" Liz asks.

CHAPTER SEVEN

My feet are kicked up on the coffee table, my laptop is resting on my thighs, and my head is propped up with a pillow. Work never looked so good.

A message pops up. It's from Nick.

"Hey, Gemma," he writes. "Would you mind if I set up a meeting with you today about the web testing? I really need some advice on what needs to happen with it. Carl is breathing down my back."

Don't do it. It will be weird.

I have to. He is my friend. Honestly, how weird can it get? It's over the computer.

"Sure," I type back.

When the meeting invite arrives, I drop my feet to the ground and lean forward over my computer. It's in twenty minutes. Who does that? Look at me. I am in leggings and an oversized T-shirt, and I haven't even brushed my hair. I accept the meeting.

Hurriedly, I run to my closet, change into something more appropriate, and run a comb through my hair.

How dare he? On my last day working from home, and now I have to put on actual clothes. Way to ruin it completely for me, Nick.

I log onto the virtual meeting, making sure I look okay in the picture of myself reflected back at me. Nick's name appears on the participants list.

"Oh, hey," he says. "I didn't know we were doing video for this."

What? There is an option *not* to do video?

"Oh, I can stop. I didn't know, I just assumed."

"No, it's okay," he says as his face appears on the screen in front of me. "Every meeting I've had this past week hasn't been on video. We just do voice." His hair is a mess, and he is wearing a T-shirt.

Damn it. I shouldn't have changed. He looks like I did.

"Oh, I canceled all of my meetings, so I didn't know."

"I noticed."

"Well, now I know for the next time the building is uninhabitable."

"Yeah, bummer that this is all over tomorrow. I was really liking working from home."

"Me too. I was just getting good at it, minus this meeting being on video that I just did to us."

"Don't worry about it. There are worse people to be on a video call with."

"Speak for yourself."

"Ouch!"

"Have you talked to Brittany? I haven't really since Fenway."

"Yeah, she messages me once in a while, just to harass me."

I smile. "Got to keep you honest."

Nick turns his head back and forth and squints his eyes. He leans forward and his face appears bigger on my screen.

"What are you doing?" I ask.

"I am trying to see your apartment."

"What? Why?"

"Because it looks tiny. Is that your bed?"

I shift my computer so my bed is out of visual range.

"Yeah, I live in a studio," I say.

"Don't be embarrassed. Look at my apartment," he says and leans out of the way of the camera. "It is tiny, too."

"What is that behind you?"

He yanks his head back into view.

"Nothing."

"That is clearly not nothing." I lean forward a little to peer into the video.

"Fine. It's a deer head."

"A deer head? Did you kill it yourself?"

"No, my grandfather gave it to me."

"Oh, that's not that weird. Can I see it?"

"Sure."

He picks up his laptop and takes me over to see the mounted head that is hanging on the wall.

"Oh, he's a pretty buck. Too bad your granddad killed him."

"I know, right?" He turns the laptop back around and looks at me. "Why aren't you more disturbed by the deer head?"

"Should I be?"

"I thought maybe."

"Well, I am from Maine. I've seen a lot of deer heads on walls. My cousin actually has a couple of them."

"That explains so much."

"Hey!"

"Just kidding. Are your parents still in Maine?"

"Yep. I kind of miss Maine. It is so much more laid back than it is here."

"I bet. Except for all those deer heads."

"Exactly. They are always keeping an eye on you."

Nick looks down and smiles. "Anyway, I need help with the web testing."

"Oh, right, you did say something about that. Let me share my screen."

"Whoa," he says once I share my desktop. "You have fifteen thousand emails in your inbox?"

"Why, is that weird?"

"Yes, that is weird, Gemma."

"I just never delete them."

"Well, you should."

I minimize my email and pull up a spreadsheet to walk Nick through line by line before I unshare my screen.

"That help?" I ask.

"Yeah…"

My head snaps around as a loud screeching noise and then a large bang echoes through my apartment.

"Gemma?" Nick says.

What the hell was that? That was far worse than a car accident. It didn't sound that close. Or did it?

"Gemma, are you okay?"

I look back at Nick, staring at me through the computer screen, as an even louder crash continues for a few seconds.

"Can you hear…"

Before I can finish my question, Nick's face disappears. My computer has lost its remote connection to my work computer.

"That can't be good," I say out loud to myself.

No, it cannot.

I try three times to regain access to my computer in the office to no avail.

Brittany texts me, "Did you lose connection?"

"Yes," I quickly type back.

Nick then texts, "Are you okay? I can't get back online."

"Yes," I write back. "I am fine. I can't get back on either."

I put my laptop onto the coffee table and lean back against the couch.

"What the hell is happening?" I say out loud to myself.

You should go look.

Go look?

Yes.

Where?

I don't know. Leave the apartment and walk towards the noise.

Right, the noise.

Sirens come from all directions and cars honk in the distance.

You should follow the noise.

Really? Be one of those people?

Yes. Do it.

But…

Do it.

No, I should stay.

But I don't.

I slip on my flipflops and take the elevator down to the street, not even thinking about my appearance. Good thing I changed for my meeting with Nick. In the distance I can hear sirens. I walk towards them on my usual route to the office building. A car alarm gets louder and louder as I approach Federal Street. A police car has blocked the street entrance, and I can see blue and red lights flashing down the street.

Go in.

No.

Go in.

No. They're not going to let me. They've blocked off the street. Look at all of those police cars. There is no one down there but emergency workers.

Fine. But I'm sure you can get a better view if you walk down Congress Street and peek in from the other side of Federal Street. Your office building is on the end. You will have a chance to see what is happening down there.

Deal.

I briskly walk by the police cruiser and turn the corner onto Congress Street. As I walk by the buildings, I try to peek in between to see if I can make out anything that is going on, but I can't. I turn the corner onto Milk Street and come back up to the end of Federal. There is not another cruiser blocking this side of the street, presumably because it is a one-way street, and traffic won't be coming in this way.

Perfect. Just quietly walk in, just a few steps.

It only takes a few for me to see what has happened. The crane that was replacing the HVAC unit on the roof of the building has collapsed and sideswiped the building on the way down. The side of the building has broken windows all the way down the side of the building, and part of the roof is flapping in the wind. There is glass all over the street. The crane has collapsed on top of three cars on the side of the road. From what I can see, no one is being put into an ambulance.

Thank goodness. Hopefully, no one is hurt.

I flashback to all the times I prayed something like this would happen, that something would happen to the building so I wouldn't have to go to work.

Oh my God, did I do this? Did I wish this into happening? Did I do this with my mind?

Shush. It's like a dream come true.

I slowly walk backwards until the building is out of sight. What do I do now? It's not like I can go back to work.

Sally's?

Walking into Sally's, I sit at a table across from Walter, who is already seated. He and Sally just stare at me.

"So?" they ask at the same time.

Before I can answer, my phone starts buzzing, and I put it to my ear. It is a robocall from my office. "There has been an incident at our office building. We are implementing our Disaster Recovery Plan. You may not be able to access your computer in the office at this time. Please do not attempt to go into the office building. We will contact you with an update. We expect to have only a short business interruption in our operations. If you are a member of the Disaster Recovery Team, you should have already received a call. We appreciate your patience and understanding in this matter. You will be hearing from us regarding our Business Continuity Plan so we can continue operations." The line goes dead.

I hang up the phone and place it on the table without saying a word.

What the hell is happening?

My phone buzzes, again. It's a text from Brittany.

"What the heck is happening?" she asks.

Sally sits down at the table with us.

"Are you okay, honey? What is happening?"

What *is* happening?

"I'm not really sure."

My phone buzzes, again. It's Carl. His group message to his department reads, "Please sit tight. We are trying to figure things out. No need to worry. Everything will be fine. I'll keep you updated."

I immediately receive another text. It's from Nick. "What the hell is happening?" he asks.

No one knows, buddy. No one knows.

No really, Gemma. They don't know. They didn't say what happened in any of the messages. No one knows, but you.

Oh, my God, McGruff.

He's fine. No one was in the building. They made all the companies work from home, remember?

Then where is my text from him? Doesn't he want to know what the hell is happening?

"Gemma?"

Oh, shit. I'm still here, sitting in silence.

"A crane collapsed. It destroyed the side of my office building."

"Oh, my God," Sally says.

"Oh, dear," Walter sighs. "Was anyone injured?"

"Not that I could see. It looks like they had blocked off Federal Street to traffic while the crane was in use. It's such a narrow street. There's no way they'd be able to get traffic by the crane, so I don't think anyone on the street was injured. And no one should have been in the building. I hope no one was injured. But the building looks a mess. The crane must have completely sideswiped the building. There was glass all over the street. The police were blocking the street, so I didn't walk down. I don't know how much damage there is."

"Are you going to be okay, honey? You look pale," Sally says.

"I'll be fine."

"I'll get you something to eat."

"Okay, thank you."

"Gemma, dear, you should text your friends back instead of staring at your fingernails," Walter says and winks at me.

I smile. "You're right. Thanks, Walter."

I quickly text back both Brittany and Nick with as much detail as I know. Sally places a sandwich in front of me and sits back down with us. We are the only three in the store.

"Everyone else ran out when all the fuss started," she says.

"How is that guy of yours?" Walter asks.

Taking a bite of my sandwich, I shrug.

Yeah, how is he? Why hasn't he texted me yet? Nick has texted me. Brittany has texted me. But not McGruff. Why the hell not? His company is bound to be in the same boat as mine.

Why don't you text him, Gemma? You can see how he is.

"Oh, speak of the devil," Walter says.

What? What devil?

I look up to see dapper, handsome, McGruff gliding over to the table. He pulls out the fourth seat of the table and sits down.

"You were talking about me?" he says, shyly smiling, his eyes sparkling.

Damn him. How dare he be so adorable.

He reaches over and grabs my hand.

"What are you doing here?" I ask.

"I was pretty sure I'd find you here since working isn't really an option right now. Plus, you've been avoiding my texts, so I thought I'd come down in person so you couldn't avoid me."

How dare his eyes smile at me.

"Did your company lose power, too?" I ask.

"Yep. Not sure when we will be able to work again. I don't think we will be back in the office soon, but they should have the computers back up and running in a day or two so that we can work from home."

Sally stands up. "I'll fix you something to eat, too."

"Thanks, Sally."

"Of course, honey."

"Do you have any more information on what happened?" Walter asks McGruff.

"From what I hear, the crane lost balance in the wind, with the HVAC unit still attached, tore up the roof of the building and started a fire, then toppled down with the unit on the end, scraping across the building as it went down, just like a wrecking ball. Does that sound right?" he asks, looking at me.

"Well, yes. I can confirm the roof and the side of the building are damaged and that the crane fell. I went down to look."

"I knew you would." He smiles.

"Well, I'll leave you two kids alone," Walter says as he stands up and pushes in his chair.

No, Walter. Don't. Don't leave me.

But he does. He winks at me, nods to McGruff, and moseys on out of the store.

Can I do the same? I can do the same thing, right? I can get up and just walk out?

No. No, you definitely cannot. Why do you even want to?

After I watch Walter walk out the door and leave me here, I turn back to McGruff who is watching me.

"What?" I ask.

He raises an eyebrow. "Nothing."

Yeah, right. There's definitely something.

"So, how does the building look?" he asks.

"Pretty bad. There were police up and down the street. My company called. They don't know when they will be back up and running."

"Same with mine," he says quietly and just looks softly into my eyes.

Nope. Stop that. Still mad.

Still mad? Really? Look at those eyes.

Yes. Still mad. We haven't even talked about the fight yet. Stacey is going to be so mad at me.

It's okay. Calm down. It's just McGruff.

He reaches over, takes my hand, and holds it.

"You know, I thought you might still be mad at me until you showed up at O'Brady's on Saturday night."

"I *am* still mad at you."

He sighs and rubs his thumb across the back of my hand.

"I know, but at least you are talking to me now."

I hold his gaze for a moment before looking down.

"What are your plans for the rest of the day?" he asks.

"I was planning to stress about work tomorrow, but I'm not sure work tomorrow is even going to happen now."

His eyes smile at me.

Damn him. Why does he always have to do that?

"Let me walk you home?"

No. Say no.

"Sure."

That was not a no.

Smiling, he looks down, shyly. "Good."

"Bye, Sally," I say.

She waves at us as we walk out the door. McGruff takes my hand and holds it gently. We walk in silence until we reach my apartment.

"I can never get over how small this place is," he says.

"I told you it was a shoebox."

"I know, but still." He notices my laptop on the coffee table. "Is this where you work from home? At the coffee table?"

"Partly. I also operate at the breakfast bar."

"Gemma, we have got to get you a desk."

I like the way he said "we."

"Okay, it's midafternoon, so what would you normally be doing?" he asks.

"Dreading the rest of the day and preparing to dread tomorrow."

"Gemma," he says and runs his hand by my ear and through my hair. "Why do you do this to yourself?"

Do I have a choice? No, I don't.

"What am I supposed to be doing? What would you be doing?"

"I would probably be getting an afternoon coffee and then cruising though the next couple of hours."

What must it actually be like to like your job?

You like your job.

Some of it. What must it be like to not be so anxious about your job?

That's a better question.

Walking over to the couch, he sits and pats the seat next to him. I comply and curl up next to him. He stretches his arm around my shoulder, and I lean my head against him.

"We need to talk," I whisper.

"Yes. We do. But can we just enjoy this moment? We can talk later."

"I'd like that."

My breathing slows, my heartbeat steadies, and I close my eyes.

CHAPTER EIGHT

I receive a text message from Carl early the next morning explaining that the system has not yet been restored and that we will have the day off, but we should be prepared to sign back on to work on Wednesday morning as if nothing has happened. We should be prepared to go to all of our scheduled meetings and not cancel them. We should be prepared to work from home just as effectively and efficiently as we would in the office building.

So, no canceling meetings?

That's all you took from that message? No. No canceling meetings.

I guess that everyone did the same thing that I did and canceled them all last week. Apparently, this time is different. He did not say when we would be going back to the office. That is the real takeaway here.

I bemuse that gem as I pull the covers back up and close my eyes.

It's okay. Just breathe. You don't have to be in the same room with him. You don't even have to see him. He's just going to be a voice, a distant voice, that you can mute if you have to. It won't be as bad as the first meeting with him. It can't be. Nothing would be as bad as that. Remember, he is just a disembodied voice. You are not there. You are fine.

I sigh and click the link to the meeting invite for my meeting with Jack. I should have just canceled it. Sure, Jack would have told Carl, but what's Carl going to do about it now? I am already scheduled to return to the daily meeting, and Carl can't just pop over to my desk and ask about it. Damn it. I should have canceled when I had the chance.

There's still time. Jack hasn't logged on yet.

I am alone in cyberspace. I don't know what's worse, being alone in a conference room waiting or being alone listening to static. No, I do know. It's definitely alone in a conference room.

Jack's name pops up in the meeting participants list, and my heartbeat quickens. I take a few deep breaths and wait. And wait. And wait.

What the crap is that dinosaur doing? Does he not know how to join a virtual meeting?

Probably not. It is Jack.

There is one click before Jack screams though the computer, "Can you hear me?"

I flinch from the decibel level.

"Yes, I can hear you."

"Finally! I've been yelling. What took you so long?"

Me? Me? Is he kidding?

"Where do you want to begin?" I ask.

"I wanted to start…"

And silence. There is just dead air. He has undoubtedly muted himself by accident.

I should say something.

No. Just ride it out. Sit in peace.

No. He will expect me to do whatever he is telling me to do that I can't hear.

"Jack," I say hesitantly. "Jack, I can't hear you. You must be on mute."

"What!" is all I hear before his name disappears from the participant list.

For the love of goodness, the man has somehow disconnected from the meeting.

I should message him and tell him.

Heck, no. Enjoy this.

His name reappears right before the screaming. "This son of a bitch!"

"Hi, Jack."

"Can you hear…" he screams before his name drops off the list, again.

I don't even know how this is possible. The man works in IT.

"Hello!" He's back.

"Hi, Jack. Are you having technical issues?"

"Yes! I am! This stupid thing!"

"Okay. Why don't we meet some other time? After you get your connection worked out."

"Good!" he yells and then drops off the call.

There is dead air again. I disconnect my end and lean back on the couch.

Well, that was exciting. Even if he did all that on purpose, I would not be mad at all. I barely had to meet with the guy. He did scream through most of the meeting, but I am pretty sure it was at his computer and not me.

You did it! You made it through your last one-on-one meeting with Jack. What will you do to celebrate?

I will lie down on the couch and pretend like it is not a work day. I will close my eyes and imagine that meeting did not even happen.

Closing my laptop, I flop down sideways on the couch and close my eyes. I can feel myself drifting off when my internal alarm clock makes my eyes flick open.

It's time for your meeting with Nick. Get ready.

Get ready? I don't need to get ready. This is as ready as I'll ever be. I will just log on and lie here on the couch. He will never know.

Nick's name pops up on the meeting list.

"Hey, Nick."

Silence.

Nope. Not on audio yet? Cool. I'm just talking to myself.

"Hey, Gemma."

"Hey, Nick."

At least no one heard you talk to yourself.

"These meetings are weird," Nick offers.

"Yeah, this must be what Raj felt like every day in our daily meetings."

"He never did video though."

"Can you see me?"

Pure panic.

Nick laughs. "No. Not this time. I can't see you unless you turn on the camera."

Thank goodness. My heart slowly returns to its normal beat.

"Why? What are you hiding over there?" Nick asks.

"Nothing!" I say way too quickly.

"Uh huh. Why don't I believe that?"

Nothing at all, just your unbrushed hair and your leggings and T-shirt. Nothing to hide at all.

"You saw my apartment last time," I deflect.

"Yes, but you've had plenty of time to hide some contraband in there."

Contraband? Me?

"Yeah, right."

"So, how was your meeting with Jack?" Nick asks. "I see it didn't run long. You were already here when I joined."

"Yeah, it was a shitshow. He couldn't join the meeting. Then he couldn't unmute himself, and then he kept getting disconnected, so we just called it quits. It was actually probably the best case scenario."

I hear Nick laughing. "Well, he'll probably be better virtually," he says.

"Probably. I can just log off or mute the whole conversation."

"Exactly."

"Today was my last day of my one-on-ones with Jack, though. With you, too. I am rejoining the daily meeting."

"You're last day of freedom, huh?"

"Unfortunately."

"What are you going to do with your last day?"

"I'm going to finish writing the requirements so everyone can pick them apart in the daily meeting."

"Sounds like a plan."

"Do you have anything you want to discuss about the web requirements today? I think we are pretty much done."

"No. I am good. Just wanted to hear your voice."

"Funny."

"When do you think we are going back to the office?" he asks.

"Honestly, I hope never."

"You never want to see me and Brittany again?"

"I can see you guys. It's everyone else I don't want to see."

And McGruff.

Shut up.

"So, you're saying that you want to plan another night where the three of us go out?"

"I'm not sure that's what I was saying."

"I am pretty sure it is. I will talk to Brittany about it."

What? No. I don't leave my apartment anymore unless I absolutely have to.

You still see Liz.

She makes me.

"Gemma? You still there?"

Oh, geez. I can't be silent in cyberspace. People will think I've just hung up on them.

You should do that, actually. It would be more fun.

"Yeah, I am here."

"Just too excited about seeing us again, huh?"

"That must be it. I am so excited I couldn't talk."

"So, what do you miss most about the office?" Nick asks.

Miss? About the office? Nothing comes to mind. And certainly nothing that I would consider to be the most.

"You know," I say. "I can't think of anything."

"I miss the air conditioning. I am sweating so bad right now."

"Oh, that's too bad. My apartment building has AC all throughout the building. If it didn't, I would probably die."

"Yeah, you get pretty sweaty in the heat, if I remember correctly."

"Hey! You guys forced me to go out to lunch in the heat. It wasn't my choice. If I had a choice, I would have stayed in the office, but no, you guys had to go out to the park and take me with you."

"Okay. Okay. I get it. We are evil friends."

"Exactly."

"Good. Now that that's cleared up, where should we go next?"

"Next? You haven't even asked Brittany yet."

"I am sure she will say yes."

"Okay, well, I don't leave my apartment anymore, so good luck dragging me out in this heat, again."

"I have resources at my disposal."

"You mean Brittany?"

Nick laughs. "Yes, she is exactly what I mean."

"Maybe we should wait until we are back in the office."

"Party pooper!"

Yes. I am. I always have been. And you know what? Right now, I am fine with it. I get to hibernate in my air-conditioned apartment where no one can see or find me.

What about McGruff?

Damn it.

Have you even talked to him lately?

No.

Don't you think you should?

I will text him after work.

Will you?

Yes. I will.

You have your appointment with Janet after work.

I will text him eventually.

He is going to San Francisco this weekend for that computer programming conference.

I know. I remember him yelling that at me outside O'Brady's.

Don't you think you should forgive him?

Just let me get through today, and I will text him later.

"Gemma?"

Shit. I am still in this meeting with Nick.

"Still here."

"Good. I thought you hung up on me."

"Not yet. Only if you make me leave my apartment."

"Oh, I am definitely going to make you come out with us."

"Okay, well it was good talking to you then. Bye!"

"Wait…" I hear him say before I hit the "Leave Meeting" button.

That was cruel.

I told him I'd hang up on him.

Well, you showed him.

Now I just have to get through the rest of the day. And know what? That isn't so bad anymore. Before, when I was in the office, it was a constant struggle to get through the day. Now, I can just sit here and casually do my work while sitting on my couch in basically pajamas.

Don't forget your Janet appointment later.

Crap. Now I have something to stress about. Thanks.

And don't forget to text McGruff later.

My heart speeds up.

Damn it. Just breathe.

Lying on my bed, my face smushed into the pillow, I open one eye and look at the clock. It's a half hour before my appointment with Janet.

You have to get up, Gemma. You have to go to the appointment. Not only did you promise Stacey that you would go, but it will actually help you. It will make you feel better.

116

It *might* make me feel better. This medication was supposed to make me feel better, too, remember? And here I am, lying lifelessly in bed before the sun has even set.

You need to roll out of bed and get up.

But I don't.

Gemma, if you don't get up now, you are going to be late. Pick up your phone, order a Road Trip, and drag your butt down to the lobby.

But I don't.

Gemma, you need to do this!

I inhale and exhale deeply.

Fine. I suppose I can go.

Rolling onto my back, I pick up my phone, order a Road Trip, and then continue to roll right out of bed. I don't even look in the mirror, I just slip my shoes on and head out the door. Just as I am getting to the elevators, the doors open, and Walter moseys out.

"Hey there, kid," he says.

I half-heartedly lift my hand to wave and half grunt in response.

"Whoa." He stops me before I silently pass him and board the elevator. He looks down at my outfit and then up to my unbrushed hair. "You going to Sally's?"

"No, I have an appointment."

"Are you okay? You seem off lately."

"Yeah. I'm fine."

I do my best to smile, but he doesn't seem convinced.

"Okay, I will see you soon, then."

I nod and step over the slit of death into the elevator. The doors close on Walter's concerned face.

Good going, Gemma. You are making Walter worried. Can't you just perk up a bit?

Perk up? Perk up!

Okay. Wrong choice of words.

How about swim? Do you need to swim?

I haven't thought about swimming in a while. It's usually what I use to convince myself to get out of a sad or indifferent mood. It's usually related to my depression.

I'm not sure this slump I am in calls for swimming. I don't feel myself sinking, not like I used to anyway. This is different. This is sloth. I don't know how to counteract this. This is new.

Jogging?

Oh, my God, no. Not even in a metaphorical sense. I can't get behind that one.

A blue Toyota pulls to the curb in front of where I am standing on the sidewalk. Without even verifying that it is my Road Trip, I open the door and get in.

"Hey, sorry, but my air conditioner is broken."

For the love of God. Why?

That is the only thing she says to me for the entire ride, and despite the fact that I am a puddle of sweat when I step out onto the curb in front of Janet's office building, I actually enjoyed the car ride. Actually, the silence.

I bloody my cuticles waiting for Janet to call me into her office. Her no nonsense office has not changed. I still have to sit across a desk from her like I'm on an interview.

She pushes her dark hair behind her ear as she pulls up my file on the laptop in front of her.

"Okay," she says, reading whatever notes she had written the last time I was in here. "We upped your dosage last time." She looks at me, assesses my unkempt appearance and glazed look in my eyes, and looks back to her notes. "You said last time that you still had a lot of anxiety. How are you feeling now?"

"Still pretty anxious."

"How are you feeling otherwise?"

"I'm tired all of the time. I get irritated easily. I sweat a lot."

Good. The abridged version, straight to the point.

"Do you feel differently since we increased the dose?"

"Yes, I feel like it's getting worse. I don't feel like myself."

"And do you feel as sad?"

As sad? Well, no, I guess this goes back to the swimming. I don't feel like I need to swim as much.

"Now that I think about it, no."

"Okay. Well, the Zoloft is helping your depression, but you say it's not helping your anxiety, and it's causing you to be irritable and tired. So, what I am thinking is that we try another SSRI. Since it's helping the depression, I want to try a different one to see if we can get your anxiety under control, too. And with less side effects. The irritability and fatigue are, more than likely, side effects of Zoloft and not a new symptom of depression."

Stacey is good at her job. She knew it. She called this one.

"So, I am thinking," Janet continues, "that we will start Celexa now. You can stop the Zoloft. You haven't been taking it long enough to have any withdrawal symptoms. I will send in a prescription for Celexa, and you can start on that immediately. I want you to make another appointment at the front desk for four weeks from now. And if you feel anything out of the ordinary, anything at all, I want you to call me immediately. Okay?"

"Okay."

Well, here I am at the beginning all over again. I am where I was two months ago.

That's not true! You even said yourself that you don't feel as depressed. That is a good thing.

Yes. But, I'd rather not feel anxious. There is nothing I can do for that. And don't say jogging. I won't do that metaphorically or literally.

What now?

Back to bed?

Really? The sun is still out. Let's go to Sally's, get something to eat, and wait for your prescription to be filled.

119

And I do. I walk in to find Walter sitting at a table by the window.

"Walter," I say. "I thought I saw you on your way back from here earlier."

"I thought I'd see if you stopped by after your appointment. I am glad I did. Sit."

"Thanks. Sally, some of the casserole please."

"Coming right up," she replies.

"You look…" Walter starts.

"It's okay. You can say that I look like crap."

"That's not what I was going to say."

"Close though."

"Maybe. You don't seem like yourself lately. And you don't leave your apartment for work anymore. I am going to try a tai chi class at Frog Pond on Saturday morning. I want you to come with me."

"Tai chi?"

"Don't let him fool you, honey," Sally says, putting a dish in front of me. "It's senior tai chi. You sit in a chair."

"Don't discourage her!" Walter says. "I want her to come with me!"

Go with Walter.

What? To senior tai chi?

Yes. It will be good for you. It helps with anxiety.

Senior tai chi? With a bunch of seniors? Doing tai chi in a chair?

Yes.

"Okay, Walter, I will go with you."

"Great. I am looking forward to it."

That makes one of us.

When I am back in my apartment, I flop down onto my couch and look at my phone.

Text him. Just get it over with.

"Hey," I type and hit send.

Hey? Really?

120

"Hey," he responds with a smiley face.

"We need to talk," I write.

Oh, my God, Gemma, right to business. Can't you talk to him for a little while? You sound so serious. You just want to talk to him about what Stacey said, right?

"I know," he says. "But I'd like to talk in person."

Tell him you're not mad at him anymore. He thinks you are still mad at him.

"Okay. When are you leaving for the conference?"

"Friday morning."

And that is it. I should text him again, say something nice. Say something funny. Say something cute.

But I don't.

CHAPTER NINE

My eyes pop open. It's 5:42 in the morning.

I have to go back to the daily meeting today.

It will be okay. You don't so much have to go as just to log on. It will be fine. You don't have to be in the room with all of them.

So, can I go back to sleep for an hour then? Maybe? Turn off my anxiety for an hour? Please?

I close my eyes and breathe deeply.

Nope. Guess not. Why would I think I'd be able to fall asleep again? That was a good joke.

Get up and get ready.

Get ready? I am planning on staying in my pajamas all day.

Okay, then make yourself some tea.

I sigh. Man, I miss coffee.

Why don't you have some?

What? No. I can't. I couldn't.

Yes, you can. You don't have to go into the office today. What's it going to hurt?

Shut up. Should I?

Yes, you should.

Yes, I should.

A broad smile stretches across my face as I roll out of bed more than an hour before I usually do. I grab a blanket off my bed, wrap up in it as I head into the kitchen, hit the button on my single serve coffeemaker, and watch the liquid brown gold drizzle into my cup. I don't even care that it is so early. I just want to curl up on the couch with my mug and sip the coffee. I love the smell. I love the taste. It's as if I've just been released from prison and can once again taste freedom.

"I missed you so much," I say out loud.

Putting my feet up, I stretch out on my couch with my freshly poured cup of coffee in hand. Work days don't get much better than this.

I hold the mug up to my nose and smell the aroma before taking my first sip. Yes. I missed this, my sweet nectar of the gods. How have I lived so long without it? How did I get through day after day without my one true love?

I take another deep breath and breathe in the beautiful smell of hot coffee.

"I love you," I say out loud, lean back on the couch, and relax with my precious contraband.

As I slowly wake up, and the clock nears eight, I waddle over to my laptop with the blanket still around me and log onto my computer. While I scroll through my emails, the meeting reminder pops up.

It's time. It's time for my triumphant return to the daily meeting. I am sure no one will even notice. Let's do this.

I click the link to the virtual meeting, and it opens the application. I am careful to hit mute and camera off before I log on. And, of course, I am the first one there. Even in the virtual world, I am always first.

Brittany's name pops up, and after five seconds I hear static and some clicking.

"Hi, Gemma!" I hear Brittany say through the computer.

I unmute myself and say, "Hey, Brittany."

"Welcome back."

"It is so good to be back."

"I am sure it is."

A few more clicks, and I see Carl's, Nick's, and Ed's name appear on the list of participants. I immediately mute myself again.

"Carl is here," Carl says.

"Hey, this is Nick."

"Ed is here."

"We'll wait a few more minutes before we get started," Carl says. "Did everyone log on okay?"

I don't respond, but I hear two yeps from Nick and Ed.

Bill's name pops up, but he doesn't announce himself.

"Just waiting on Jack now," Carl says.

My nemesis.

As his name finally appears, my heart rate starts to increase.

What the hell are you doing? You are at home wrapped up in a blanket. There is no need for this anxiety.

I take a few deep breaths and close my eyes. I can do this. I am not even there. I can make it through this meeting.

"Jack," he grunts to announce himself.

Calm down.

"Great," Carl says. "Why don't we go over some of the things Jack pointed out to me in the requirements?"

What? What things? He literally helped me put them together. We had meetings just the two of us. He couldn't bring these things up then? He has to do this in front of the whole class?

"Jack, will you share your desktop?"

Jack grunts again. I can only assume that is a yes.

"Can you see my desktop?" he asks.

No. I can't.

Three people say no at the same time.

"Oh, I forgot to share."

Forgot to share? How is that possible? He just told you to share.

Jack finally pulls up the requirements and starts rambling on and on.

Bling. A message from Brittany pops up. It reads, "I bet you missed being in these meetings. What a great way to start back up again."

I write back, "Yep. I truly missed this."

"At least, now we can talk to each other during it. Should we add Nick to our convo?"

Nick? No. Why should we?

But it's too late. She has already added him.

"Welcome back, Gemma," he writes.

"Thanks, Nick. It's like my life was incomplete without this horrible meeting."

Bill's voice blares through the speaker. "Can you reshare? I think we lost your desktop. Anyone else?"

"Yes, me too," Carl says.

Shit. What has Jack been saying about my beautiful requirements?

Pay attention, Gemma.

Jack puts his desktop back on the screen. Before he speaks, someone starts typing loudly, and it is broadcast out over the meeting.

"Whoever is typing, can you go on mute?" Carl asks.

The typing abruptly stops.

"Bill," Nick writes in the chat. "Had to be Bill."

"Of course," Brittany responds.

"Nick?" Carl asks. "Nick, what do you have to add about the state tax issue?"

"Sorry, I was on mute," Nick says. "I fixed the code. It's moving into QA this afternoon."

"Great."

Nick types into the chat, "I was not on mute. I just wasn't listening."

"Join the club," I write. "I don't think I've heard one thing Jack has said about my requirements."

"Don't you have to send out meeting notes?" Nick writes.

"Shit. I forgot that was my responsibility in these meetings," I write.

"Don't worry. I've got you covered," Nick writes.

"Your computer froze," Ed says in the meeting. "Can you reshare, again?"

"Jeepers," Brittany writes. "Get your shit together, Jack."

125

This is so much better than real life meetings.

This *is* real life.

You know what I mean. I mean, sitting there, slowly dying inside while people argue around me. This way is so much better.

"Gemma?" Carl asks. "Can you update those?"

I have a feeling it wasn't the first time he has asked.

I unmute myself. "Sorry, I was on mute," I say. "Sure, I can update those."

If I ever figure out what updates those are.

"Hey!" Nick writes. "That was my line."

"You can't take credit for it," I write. "It's a classic."

"Just don't go using it all the time now."

But I will. I will use it any chance I get because I know that I cannot for the life of me, pay attention in any meetings, especially those in virtual reality.

My phone buzzes, and I look down. There is a text from McGruff. I wonder what he is doing. Oh, my God. He is flying out to San Francisco today. I should have texted him first. I am such a jerk.

"Just wanted to say hi before I board," he says.

"Hey, I hope you have a good flight," I type out. "Text me when you land."

He responds immediately with a kissy face emoji.

I hit the first emoji that I can find and hit send.

Oh, my God, Gemma. You just sent a thumbs up emoji. What are you doing? You can't reply to a kissy face with a thumbs up. Send something else.

But I don't.

You really stink at life, don't you, Gemma?

Yes, I do. Just one more thing to talk to my therapist about tonight, I guess.

"Gemma?" Carl asks.

For the love of God, girl, can you ever pay attention?

"What is he asking?" I quickly type into the chat.

"Update the vehicle VIN field in the requirements," Brittany types back.

"Yes," I unmute myself and say, "I can get that done today."

Can you though? Look at you. You are wrapped up in blanket and barely paying attention to anything.

It's not much different than being in the office, except now I have a blankie.

"That's right!" Jack yells.

I flinch and then sigh. Even in cyberspace, he can still cause so much anxiety.

Good thing you are going to see Stacey tonight. You have much to discuss.

Like the fact that I still haven't talked to McGruff, and now he's across the country.

Here I am, back at Stacey's office, waiting for my hot Friday night plans to start.

Why do you always say that? You could have hot Friday night plans with McGruff. You do have that option now.

Well, technically McGruff is out of town, so I can't have hot Friday night plans with him tonight.

Okay, well, every other Friday night you can. Yet, you either cancel or come here. Why is that?

"Gemma?"

I look up from my bloody cuticles to see Stacey standing in the room.

"I'm glad you made it in two weeks in a row," she says as we walk down the hall and into her room.

Was that a joke?

"The first thing I want to ask about," she says as we both sit in our respective seats, "is your follow up with Janet. How'd that go?"

You should tell her you canceled. You can joke, too.

"She is switching my medication. She is stopping the Zoloft, and I am going to try Celexa."

"Good. I am glad she is changing it."

I nod.

"What else has been happening? Have you joined the daily meeting again?"

"Yes."

"How has that been?"

"Not so bad, actually."

"Oh," she seems surprised. "Why is that, you think?"

Of course, she is surprised. You spent weeks telling her how it was the bane of your existence and how you hated every single second of it.

"Did you see the crane collapse on the news? That was my building."

"Oh, wow. Yes, I did see that."

"I've been working from home for a week and a half. It was supposed to be only a few days while they fixed the HVAC system, but now they don't know how long that's going to be."

"Why do I sense you aren't happy about it?"

"Oh, I am. I am over-joyed at the fact that I get to work from home. It's so much easier on me and my anxiety."

"But?"

"But I feel bad that I am so happy about it when other people were hurt in the collapse. The building and the other buildings it fell on were seriously damaged. It caused major damage and problems for so many people. Most people don't want to work from home, or they hate it. And here I am, loving life. It doesn't seem right."

"I see. You don't think that good things can come from bad situations?"

"I guess they can, but I still feel guilty."

"Why do you? It's not your fault that this happened."

Are we sure about that? I did wish for it every single day of my life for the past five years.

"I know, but other people are miserable."

"You aren't allowed to be happy if other people aren't?"

"I don't know. I guess I am."

"Yes. You are. You absolutely are. You were miserable for far too long while everyone else was happy. You were miserable while no one else cared. You deserve to be happy without feeling guilty, even if other people aren't. No one felt guilty over you. You should be happy."

Damn. She's good. She is right. I was miserable, and no one even gave me a thought. I should be happy about working from home while I can be. I deserve to be happy.

Yes, you do! You go, girl!

"Tell me about working from home."

"Oh, it's so great. I don't have to see anyone. If people are fighting, I am not physically stuck between them. I can just close my eyes and try to relax. I can even mute them!"

"That sounds great."

"It is. And that's not the best part. Since most of my meetings aren't on video, I get to work in basically my pajamas every day. I don't even have to brush my hair if I don't want to."

Stacey laughs. "That sounds great."

"It really is. I'm going to miss it when I have to go back."

"Don't do that."

"Do what?"

"Already think about it being over. Be in the moment. Enjoy the present. Sure, this may end soon, but it hasn't yet, and you are happy. Just enjoy it while it's here."

Damn. She is so good. You really do need to do that more often. Just enjoy the moment.

"Have you talked to Nate?"

Moment over.

"I did a little. He is out of the state now on a business trip."

"I remember you telling me that. Did you get to talk about why he needs control and feels out of control with you?"

"Only a little. He said he'd call me when he is settled. And we will talk about it then."

"Okay. Great. Well, we are out of time. Same time next week good for you?"

"Actually, can we not do Friday anymore? Maybe Thursday?"

"Let me see. Yes, I can fit you in at this time on Thursday."

"That is perfect."

Look at you trying to make time for McGruff.

That is not what I am doing.

Then who are you making time for then?

CHAPTER TEN

There is a quiet, yet assertive, knock on my door.

Oh, my God. This is actually happening. Why did I agree to go to senior citizen tai chi?

You didn't agree. Walter is forcing you to go. Just don't answer the door.

I can't do that to Walter. He's Walter. I can't make him go to tai chi by himself. He probably doesn't even know how to call a Road Trip. I am going.

Slowly opening the door, I see Walter standing in the doorway with his hands behind his back.

"For a minute, I didn't think you were going to open the door," he says.

"I thought about it."

"You ready?"

"Yep. Let me just grab my purse."

"Do you know how to call one of those Road Trip things?"

"Yes. I will call us a car."

"Good. Tell them to pick us up at Sally's. I want a coffee first."

We make our way down the elevator, out of the building, and into Sally's. She looks over at us as we ding through the door.

"Well, aren't you two the cutest things I've ever seen."

"Well, I know Walter is," I say as I look down at my oversized T-shirt, leggings, and sneakers.

Walter is in khaki shorts and a baby blue polo shirt. He could probably be a plus-age model if he wanted to be.

"Here's your coffee, Walter. What can I get for you, honey?" Sally asks me.

I can't do this without caffeine. I don't know how I exist without it. I should have disintegrated by now or something.

Get a tea. Black. That's not so bad. You can deal with a little caffeine over the weekend. You'll be fine. It's not like you have to go to any meetings today.

No, I want the big guns.

"You know what, Sally? I'll take a coffee."

"Coffee? You sure, honey?"

"She wants coffee. Give her a coffee," Walter says.

"Thanks, Walter. Yes, I think I'll be fine for one Saturday morning. Besides, I am going to need as much caffeine as I can get for this."

"It's going to be fine," Walter says. "Besides, you are young. You can do this. I probably can't."

"Walter," I say, "It's senior tai chi. It is geared towards people your age."

"All right. Let's get this show on the road," he says.

"Have fun, you two," Sally says.

Our Road Trip is waiting outside by the curb. I open the door to the café for Walter and then wave at Sally as I walk through. The car brings us around the Common on Beacon Street and drops us off as close to Frog Pond as we can get. I walk slowly next to Walter until we approach the tai chi class.

There are chairs lined up across the grass and facing Frog Pond. The pond is just a shallow wading pool with a spray fountain in the middle. The pool is usually crowded in the summer, but it's too early for that. The only people around are morning walkers and our tai chi class.

The pond freezes over in the winter, and people enjoy ice skating in the colder months. Two large human sized statues of frogs overlook the pond. From the back, it looks as if they are holding court, but one is fishing and the other is bored and waiting for his friend to stop. Or that is my impression and what I imagine is going through his frog mind.

132

As we slowly approach, the instructor, who is a man in his forties, walks up to us. He is barefoot and wearing flowing cotton pants and a T-shirt.

"Welcome," he says. "Please, sit where you like."

Me too? I can just sit here with all these people Walter's age?

What did you expect? This is why you are here, isn't it?

Should I stand, though? I feel like I should stand.

Look, the instructor has a chair too. It would be weird if you stood.

"Please, sit," the instructor says to me and motions to the chair next to Walter's.

As I sit, I look over at Walter.

"This will be good for both of us," he says.

I don't know about that.

Maybe it will. Remember chair yoga? You didn't think you would like that, but you did.

And I never did it again.

Doesn't mean you didn't like it. You didn't have the opportunity to go to another class. Maybe you and Walter can go to these more often.

Whoa. Don't get too far ahead. I don't even know if I like this yet.

You would do it for Walter. Plus, it's supposed to be good for anxiety.

The chairs fill up and the instructor walks in front of us and turns his back on Frog Pond.

"We are going to start with some simple twists at the waist. So put your hands on your hips, and we are just going to twist to the left. And then twist to the right. All right. Good. A few more. Okay, good. Now mirror what I do."

I look over to my left and then to my right and see a couple dozen senior citizens waving their hands over their heads.

Why do I do these things to myself? Why am I at senior citizen tai chi waving my hands in the air and doing the bow and arrow? Why didn't I wear some sort of disguise so I wouldn't be recognized?

This class isn't too bad. Sure, you are the only person below the age of seventy, but it is kind of relaxing. Just breathe and follow along.

I take a deep breath and repeat what the instructor does. I have to say, some of these seniors are quite good at this. Focusing on my breath, I breathe in and out. Eventually, I start feeling relaxed. I keep breathing slowly. My shoulders relax, the tension in my neck disappears, and my body feels light.

Look at you. You are enjoying this.

"And that wraps up class for today," the instructor says.

What? How? We just got here. How is the class over already?

Did you fall asleep?

No! Did I?

"Did you have fun, kid?" Walter looks over and asks me as he stands up from his chair.

"I did, actually. Did you?"

"I did, too. Can you call the car service?"

"Yes, I can take care of that."

"Good. I will have plenty of time before Josh shows up."

"Oh yeah! He is coming today!"

"Yes, I am very happy. I haven't seen him since last summer."

Slowly walking towards the street, we take our time getting to the curb to wait for our car.

"I hope you get to meet him," Walter says.

"I hope so, too."

After I get home, I spend the rest of the day alternating between napping on the couch and dragging my butt and laundry down to the basement. Why does doing laundry have to be so exhausting?

You could start jogging. It might make you feel better and less exhausted just doing laundry.

How dare that even be suggested.

I have a half hour to get back to my apartment, get changed, and go out to meet Liz. Opening the dryer door, I pile my clean and dry laundry into my basket. Yawning, I stroll out of the laundry room and push the button for the elevator. It opens. I enter and close my eyes for the ride up from the basement.

Ding. My eyes pop open. I've stopped in the lobby.

No. This was supposed to be a solo ride, sir. Please turn around and get out.

A man in his forties or fifties steps in, looks at me leaning against the back of the elevator propping up my laundry, and smiles. He turns and stands with his back to me. I can see an earpiece on his ear in case he gets a call. His hair is slicked back, and he is wearing expensive looking slacks and a button-down shirt. He seems extremely confident, and he is very intimidating. My heart beats faster.

Calm down. It's just a stupid stranger. Why are you getting so anxious? It's not like he's going to talk to you.

I've never seen this guy before. I wonder if he just moved in. He seems kind familiar somehow. His smile, maybe?

The door opens on my floor, and the man gets out before me.

What? He's on my floor? This can't be right. I would have noticed someone so self-assured and intimidating before now.

I slowly walk out of the elevator and stop at the turn and look left down the hall where the stranger is walking. He stops and knocks on a door. It's Walter's door! He's visiting Walter! That must be his son!

I am still gawking when he's let into Walter's apartment, and he turns to look at me. Shit. I turn right, stumble over my feet, and drop my laundry basket onto the floor.

Great work, Gemma. Now Walter's son thinks you are a creep.

Picking up my laundry, I swiftly walk back to my apartment and drop the basket next to my closet. I will deal with the folding and hanging later. Quickly changing, I look in the mirror and sigh. When will the bags under my eyes disappear? I smooth out my hair and step into my heels.

All right. Here goes nothing.

There's still time to cancel.

Really? Liz would kill me.

I ride the elevator down to the lobby. When the door opens, I see Walter and his son standing by the door.

Crap. What do I do?

They both turn and look at me.

You can't run away now. They both saw you.

No. I still can. There's still time.

Walter waves.

And time is up.

Begrudgingly, I walk over and stand awkwardly next to them.

"Gemma! I'd like you to meet my son, Josh."

Josh reaches out and shakes my hand.

"Joshua," he corrects his father.

"It's Josh," Walter replies and winks.

"It's nice to meet you," I say.

"You, as well. I've heard a lot about you."

"Oh, boy."

Josh smiles. "No, it's all good stuff."

"Are you headed out?" I ask.

"Yes," Walter says. "Josh just got in and is starving, so we're going out to dinner."

"Just got here?" I ask, as if I didn't already know. Why did I ask that?

"Yep," Josh says. "I may have run into you on my way into the building a little while ago. I had to take a work call and didn't want to bother my dad, so I went outside."

"You met?" Walter asks.

"Oh, no," I say. "It was just in the elevator."

"She was keeping an eye out for you, Dad. Making sure I wasn't a danger."

136

Yep. He definitely saw me staring at him. Nice first impression, Gemma.

I smile awkwardly.

"Are you meeting Liz?" Walter asks me.

"Yes."

"Good."

"Why don't you have dinner with us one night this week?" Josh asks.

What? No. Why would he ask me that? I'm clearly a creep. No need to be nice to a creep, now is there?

"Yes! Please do!" Walter exclaims.

Damn. Now Walter is excited.

"Ummm..." I hesitate.

"It will be good for you," Walter says. "It's no good for such a young woman to be cooped up in her apartment all day every day. You don't even leave to go to work anymore."

"I..."

"You are coming," Walter says.

Josh smiles. "You are coming," he repeats.

"Okay. I guess I am coming."

"Good," Walter says.

A blue sedan pulls up in front of the lobby door.

"Well, that's our ride," Josh says. "It was very nice meeting you. I will see you later, I am sure." He smiles again.

"See you later, Gemma," Walter says.

"Bye."

I watch Josh open the car door for his father, close it once he's inside, and then walk around to the other side.

Shit. I guess I have to go to dinner with them.

Yes, yes you do.

Once I arrive at Flannery's, I walk in and scan the seats at the bar. She's not there. I look at all of the tables. Not there, either. Pulling out my phone, I check to see if she has sent me a cancellation text. There's none.

What? Did I beat her here? That never happens.

Slowly, I approach the bar, pull out a chair, sit, and rest my elbows on the bar. Greg comes immediately over.

"What?" he asks. "Are you alone tonight?"

"No. I'm just here first."

"What?"

"I know, right? I'm confused, too."

"I don't know what to do. I guess I'll make your drink."

"Seems logical."

"I'm bummed. Liz usually gives me the dirt on you before you get here."

"Hey!"

"Don't hey me. Hey her. Look, there she is."

Before I can turn to look, she is pulling out the chair next to me and sitting down.

"What are you doing here first?" she asks.

"I know. It has confused us all."

Greg places my drink in front of me, points and winks at Liz, and then goes to make hers.

"By the way," I say. "Greg tells me that you tell him dirt about me before I get here?"

"Only when he asks."

"Which is all the time," Greg butts in.

I look at her and raise my eyebrows.

"What? It's just Greg," she says.

"Yeah, it's just Greg," Greg echoes.

"Okay, okay," I say.

Greg smiles broadly and walks away.

"So, what's new?" I ask.

"Not a whole lot. Brett's parents are visiting tomorrow, so that should be a blast."

"Your in-laws aren't that bad. They could be so much worse. They've always been nice to me."

"I know." She takes a sip of her drink. "What's new with you? Have you talked to Nate?"

"He's in San Francisco. I saw him on Monday after the crane collapsed, but I haven't seen him since. Since we aren't going into the building, I didn't see him all week. I think he's been kind of avoiding me for a while."

"You mean giving you space."

"I don't know. It doesn't seem like he wants to talk to me either."

"Give it time. It will work out."

"Yeah…"

"Did you leave your apartment at all this week?"

"Well, on Monday to see the crane, Wednesday to see Janet, and Friday after work."

"Gemma, you need to get outside more."

"What? That was three out of five days. And it's been disgustingly hot most of the time. This is the only chance I'm going to get to hibernate like this when I'm not taking vacation days. I have to savor it."

"What about today? Did you go out?"

"Ugh. Walter made me go to senior tai chi."

"Senior tai chi!" Greg yells from a few steps over.

"Yep. Senior tai chi," I say.

"That's amazing," Liz says. "How was it?"

"Despite the fact that I was completely humiliated doing chair tai chi with a bunch of elderly people in the middle of the Common, it was actually kind of relaxing."

"Yeah, it's supposed to be good for anxiety," Liz says.

"So I hear. You know, I found this great herbal blueberry tea. It's kind of soothing."

"Who are you right now?"

"Don't worry. I have been sneaking coffee."

"Gemma!"

"I know, but I'm not in the office, so I figure it's okay."

"Yeah, but it's going to be that much harder when you go back to the office and stop again."

I sigh. "Yeah…"

"You said you saw Janet this week?"

I sigh, again. "Yep, she is changing my meds. I am at square one…*again*."

"Don't be discouraged. This is a process, not a miracle cure."

"Ugh. Don't remind me. I hate this process."

"It will be okay. You just have to stick with it. Things will turn around."

"I hope you are right."

There's a tap on my shoulder, and I turn. Barry is standing between our chairs.

"Hello, ladies. Would you like to play darts?"

Liz looks at me. I can tell she wants to.

"Oh, fine," I say.

"Yes!" Liz shouts.

"Gemma, you're on my team. Liz, you're on Billy's team," Barry says.

Great. How did I know those team assignments were coming?

We pick up our drinks and relocate to the table near the dart board.

"Hey, Billy."

"Hey, ladies, glad you are playing tonight."

That makes one of us.

Just try to have fun, would you? You are in a good place right now. You are still working from home. You've started to drink coffee, again. And you are out with your best friend right now. Try to think positively.

Barry hands me the darts. "Your turn," he says.

I take them and square off in front of the dart board. Out of the corner of my eye, I can see Liz chatting with Billy.

Just breathe. You are in a good place, physically and metaphorically. Just breathe. Everything will fall into place.

"All right. Here goes nothing."

CHAPTER ELEVEN

What am I going to do about McGruff?

What do you mean? What is there to do about McGruff?

I need to talk to him, and he still hasn't called me.

You could call him, you know? That's how phones work.

"Gemma?" Carl's voice echoes through my computer, "Can you do that today?"

Shit.

"Yes, I can," I say and mute myself.

"Can you really?" Brittany types in the chat.

"I doubt it. I am not even sure what I am supposed to do."

"You got this," she writes.

"If only," I respond.

"If only this meeting would end," Brittany replies.

"If only this job would end," I respond.

"Oh boy. When you get like this, I would usually make you go out to lunch with me," she responds.

"It's okay. I am fine."

"Right. Since it has been a couple of weeks since I've seen you two in person," Nick writes, "I propose that we all get together Friday after work for a happy hour."

What? Leave my apartment? To see coworkers? I was hoping he would have forgotten about planning a night out.

You and Brittany are definitely friends. I would not say you are just coworkers.

What about Nick? We are just coworkers.

You don't think that you two are friends now? You chat all the time.

Brittany is usually there. Plus, there was that awkward situation in the conference room that one time.

What, that old thing? You kept saying that it didn't even happen. And he hasn't brought it up at all.

True. I'm sure he's forgotten about it, too. He must have been having an off day. We have both mutually forgotten it even happened.

Then you should go out with them.

Leave my apartment? I don't do that anymore. Not voluntarily, anyway.

Well, Brittany will probably make you, so it won't be voluntary.

"Yes, I'm in!" Brittany writes.

I know they are waiting for me to respond. They always wait for me to respond. I can mentally picture both of their heads turning to look at me. Why can't they just move on with their lives like normal people? I have to respond.

"Sure," I type.

Sure? That's all you can muster is a sure?

Well, I really don't actually want to go. So yes, a sure is all I can muster.

"Yes!" Brittany writes. "We got her!"

"Awesome!" Nick writes. "She could sense us both staring at her through cyberspace."

"Where shall we go?" Brittany asks.

"I know you live in Somerville," Nick says, "so let's go somewhere in Davis Square. You can tell us a good spot, Brittany, right?"

"Yes! That sounds good to me," Brittany says.

Damn it all to hell. First, I agreed to go out with them, and now I have to go to Somerville?

It's really not that far. It's not like you have to drive. You take a Road Trip everywhere you go. You don't even have a car.

"Gemma? That okay with you?" Nick asks.

No. Say no. Say you changed your mind and that you can't make it out on Friday, after all. You are terribly sorry, but you have to sit on your couch and try and fail to find something to watch for forty-five minutes just to watch something you've already seen. You are very sorry, but you cannot go out ever again. Kindly let them know that they will never see you again in person.

"Yeah, that's fine," I write.

Why do you do this? Why do you agree to things you clearly don't want to do? Why don't you just tell them no? Tell them all no. Tell every single person in the entire universe no.

"What time do you think? Six? Is that good for happy hour?" Nick asks.

"Sounds good to me," Brittany says.

What about you, Gemma? Does that sound good to you now that you are stuck going?

"Sure," I type.

Again with sure. Just say no. What will McGruff say when he finds out?

When he finds out what? That I'm going out with my friends?

That you are going out with Nick. And see, you do think they are your friends.

I'm going out with Brittany.

And Nick.

Shut up about Nick. We have both unconsciously agreed never to speak of that awkward encounter in the conference room ever again.

You're calling it an encounter now?

"Great!" Nick writes.

"So," Carl's voice says, "Nick, can you work on that soon?"

"Oh, shit," Nick writes. "What is he talking about?"

Shit if I know. I forgot we were even in this meeting.

"Defect about the VINs," Brittany writes.

"Lifesaver," Nick writes back before saying aloud, "Yes, I plan on having that done and promoted to QA by Monday. Tuesday at the latest."

"Perfect," Carl responds.

"Is that true?" Brittany writes.

"I will make it true," Nick responds.

"And, Gemma," Carl says, "You will make the updates that Jack talked about?"

Shit. What the hell? Why does he have so many updates? Crap. I was not listening. I have no idea what updates he was talking about.

"I'll fill you in," Brittany writes before I even say anything in the chat.

What would I do without her?

I unmute myself. "Yep," is all I say and then immediately mute myself again.

"I hate this meeting," I write.

"Can't wait to read your summary of today's meeting," Nick writes.

Damn it, Gemma. Why do you never pay attention? You're not even physically there, and you can't pay attention in this meeting.

"Don't worry," Nick responds to my silence. "It will be a group effort today."

"Agreed," Brittany writes.

"Thanks, guys."

"You can buy us both a beer on Friday to thank us," Nick writes.

Damn it. I still have to go to that?

You literally just agreed to it like ten minutes ago.

I was hoping they wouldn't remember.

Oh, they remember. And you are going. Brittany will make sure of it.

Now, I just need to get through the rest of the day without falling asleep.

And I do. I close my laptop and flop down onto the couch. My eyes close, and I drift off to sleep.

My phone buzzes on the coffee table. I sit straight up when I see McGruff's name as it rings.

Damn it. A video chat? What the hell? I look like crap.

145

Just smooth out your hair. You'll be fine.

But...

You have to answer it.

But...

Answer it.

I swipe right and his beautiful face appears on my phone.

He smiles. "You answered."

How dare he have such a beautiful smile.

"Apparently."

"You look good."

Liar. I do not look good.

"I doubt that."

"You shouldn't. You always look good."

Flattery will get you nowhere.

"How was your flight?"

That's right. Change the subject.

"All in all, not bad. We had some turbulence, but it was over quick."

"How's the hotel? Looks nice."

"Yeah? You like it? The hotel is amazing. It's huge. I even have a view of the harbor."

"Shut up."

"See."

He walks over to the window and turns the camera so I can see the view.

"Shut up," I say again.

When he turns the camera back, he is smiling. "The conference has been pretty cool so far, too."

"Yuck."

He laughs. "Shut up."

I smile.

"Apple is going to give a presentation this week," he says.

"No way."

"I'm serious. It's pretty cool for a computer programming conference."

"I guess if you like that sort of thing."

"I do."

"I know. You would have become a black hat hacker if you could have."

"Exactly."

Why do his eyes have to sparkle like that?

Do not let him dazzle you like that.

"So how was your weekend?" he asks. "Didn't miss me too much I hope."

"Walter made me go to senior tai chi with him on Saturday morning. Stop laughing."

"Sorry. At Frog Pond?"

"Yep."

"How did that go?"

"Well, despite feeling like a ninety-year-old woman, it actually wasn't that bad."

"Did you sit?"

Why is he doing this to me?

"Yes."

A stupid grin spreads across his face. "I wish I could have seen that. My Gemma sitting doing tai chi with a bunch of senior citizens."

I hate that he's making fun of me, but I love that he just called me his Gemma.

"It was very relaxing. You should come with us someday."

"You're going again?"

Damn.

"Maybe. I'm not ruling it out."

"Well, I would love to go to chair tai chi with you and Walter."

"Damn straight."

"How is Walter?"

"His son is in town."

"What! I'm missing it?"

"Yep. I met him and everything."

"So jealous."

"You should be."

"What's he like?"

"He's very Wall Street. He had an earpiece in his ear the whole time in case he got a phone call mid conversation. He's very nice, but he still scares the crap out of me."

"Why?"

"He is so confident and successful."

"He is Walter's son. How scary can he be?"

"Good point."

"How long is he going to be around?"

"He is leaving Friday, so you will miss him."

"Damn it."

"I know."

"Are you going to see them again?"

"They asked me to dinner on Wednesday."

Which I am sure will be awkwardly silent because I don't talk, which will be compounded by the fact that Josh scares me.

"And are you going?"

Damn it. He's just like Liz.

"Yes."

"Did you say yes, or is Walter making you?"

Damn it.

"Walter is making me."

"Of course, he is. Good for Walter."

"Stop smiling."

"Never."

I smile and then curse his existence.

"I'm glad you're not mad at me anymore. I've missed you."

Tell him you missed him, too. Tell him.

"I've missed you, too."

His eyes are so dazzling.

"Look, we need to talk about the night at O'Brady's," he says.

Dazzle over. Do we really need to talk about it?

Yes.

Do we really?

Yes.

Fine.

"Okay."

"I felt like I was losing control. Like I was losing you somehow. And I lashed out, and I am sorry. The fact was, I wasn't losing you until I did that."

"I'm sorry, too. I know I'm not the easiest person to deal with all the time."

"No, it's not that. And you aren't difficult. I know you are dealing with a lot right now, and I understand that."

Ask him why he feels out of control. Ask him why he needs control.

But I don't. There is a knock on his hotel door.

"I'm sorry. I have to go. Some of the guys are going out to dinner tonight. I will call you soon, okay?"

"Okay."

He pauses for a second and smiles. "I miss you," he says before he ends the call, and his face disappears from the screen.

"I miss you, too," I say to my phone.

CHAPTER TWELVE

There's still time to turn around.

I'm standing in front of Walter's door. There is no time to turn back.

Yes, there is. You haven't knocked. No one has seen you. You can still go home.

Walter would be crushed.

It's going to be a silent and awkward dinner. They will be thankful you didn't show up.

Hesitantly, I raise my hand and knock twice on the door. I hear a bit of a commotion, and then the door swings open.

"Hi, Gemma," Josh says.

"Hi, Josh...ua"

He smiles. "Come on in."

He is wearing khaki pants and a polo shirt. His casual look is way dressier than anything I've worn lately.

"Ah, Gemma!" Walter says. "Welcome!"

See. He is so happy. I couldn't let him down.

"Hey, honey," Sally says, walking into the room from the kitchen holding a glass of wine.

"Sally! I didn't know you'd be here."

"Yep. I shut down early. I couldn't pass up the chance to meet Walter's son."

"You'd think I was a celebrity or something," Josh says.

"You are to us," Sally says.

Walter's apartment is a lot bigger than mine. For one, he actually has a bedroom. And two, he has a kitchen, and it is big enough for a table. We gather at it now.

"I misjudged," Walter says. "The food is done early. I hope you all don't mind eating right away."

"Not at all," I say.

"Would you like some wine, Gemma?" Josh asks.

Of course, I do. I thought you'd never ask.

"Yes, please."

He fills a glass and places it in front of me on the table.

"Josh is kind of a wine snob, so it's the good stuff," Walter says.

"Dad!"

"What?" Walter smirks.

"Okay. I do like my wine."

"Walter is right. This is very good," Sally says.

"Only the best for my dad and his two favorite ladies."

Oh, my God. How cute is that? He's not nearly as scary as I thought he'd be.

Of course, he's not. He's Walter's son, and Walter is adorable.

We all settle around the table and load our plates with the meatloaf and green beans that Walter has cooked.

"Walter, I didn't know you could cook so well," Sally says.

"I can when I want to," Walter replies. "But I usually don't want to. Plus, Josh is a big help."

"I barely did anything but pick out the wine." He winks at his dad.

Oh, my God. How cute is that? He winks just like his dad does.

"My dad tells me that you all met at your café, Sally. Is that right?"

"Yep. This one over here," she points at me, "was a regular customer before Walter moved in, but she never said more than two peeps to me." She looks at me and smiles. "And then Walter started showing up and one day invited Gemma to sit with him. And the rest, as they say, is history."

"You just sat with a random old man?" Josh asks me and grins at his dad.

"He wasn't completely random," I say. "I had seen him coming and going from the apartment building. I knew he lived on my floor. He would always smile and wink at me."

"Right," Josh says. "Who doesn't trust an old man that winks?"

Walter shakes his head.

"I mean, look at that face," I respond. "Who wouldn't trust it? Even if it is winking at you."

Josh laughs. "I guess that is true," he says.

I take a swig from my glass of wine.

Look at you making big city Josh laugh. Tonight isn't as bad as you thought it would be.

"Are you still working from home, honey?" Sally asks me.

"Yep. Still don't know when I'm going back."

"You work from home?" Josh asks. "What do you do?"

"I work at an insurance company as a business analyst. The office building is a few blocks over. It was damaged when a crane collapsed, so we've all been working from home."

"What do you do, Joshua?" Sally asks.

Thank goodness Sally is here. My nightmares of a silent dinner won't come to pass.

"I'm an investment banker."

"I bet it's all business in New York City," she replies.

"Yes. It definitely is. I wear a suit to work every day. It feels funny not to be wearing one now. How do you enjoy having your own business?"

"Oh, I love it. I love the people. But…" She looks at me and then at Walter. "I didn't want to have to break this to you tonight, but I am planning on shutting down starting at two o'clock from now on. I barely get any customers for dinner besides the two of you."

Everyone is silent until Walter says to me, "Don't worry I'll cook for you."

I can see Sally and Josh smiling.

"Walter, that's not necessary," I say.

He winks at me. "Of course, you've got Nate, now. Where is he anyway?"

"He's at a conference in San Francisco."

"Oh, that's right. He did mention that."

"So, Joshua," Sally says, "your daughter couldn't come out to visit with you?"

"No. She's with her mother this week. I will have to get her out here to visit soon." He looks pointedly at his dad.

What is that look for?

"Yes, you do," Walter says. "I haven't seen her in person for ages."

"I know. I know. Julia misses you, too."

"Of course, she does. I'm great."

"I think we can all drink to that," Sally says.

We all raise our glasses, and I take another swig of wine.

"You have a daughter, too?" Josh asks Sally.

"Yes, she's in college. I don't know how she got that old," Sally replies.

"Yeah. My Julia is only twelve, and I feel like she was just a baby," Josh responds.

"They grow up so fast," Sally says.

"Yes, they do," Walter replies.

"Gemma, more wine?" Josh asks.

What, does he think I am a lush?

I mean, probably. You just downed your wine.

"Yes, please. Thank you, Josh…ua."

See, this isn't nearly as bad as you thought it would be. Josh…ua is very nice.

If only I didn't stumble over his name.

He doesn't seem to care. Aren't you glad that you came?

Yes, I am. And this wine is really good.

"I'm glad you like it."

What? Can he read my mind?

No, he can't. He can just see you guzzling it, like the lady that you are.

Shut up.

The evening winds down, and Sally is helping Walter wash the last of the dishes. Josh walks me to the door.

"It was very nice getting to know you," he says.

"Yes, you too. This was fun."

Josh opens the door, and I step into the hall.

"I am glad that I met you on this trip," he says.

I turn back around.

"You remind me so much of my mother. I can see why he took a shine to you."

He smiles and closes the door.

Walter's wife? I remind him of Walter's wife? That is so sweet.

After standing there dumbfounded for a few moments, I turn to walk down the hall before Sally comes out and finds me still standing here.

Ugh. I should not have had so many glasses of wine last night. My head is killing me, and I barely have the energy to drag myself out of bed.

Groggily, I shuffle over to the coffee table, pick up my laptop, shuffle back, and get back into bed. I pull the covers up over me, place the computer on my lap, and hit the join meeting button. Closing my eyes, I wait for others to join. I hear the dings of people joining, but I don't bother open my eyes until I hear Carl's voice.

"Okay. I think we have a quorum."

I've already missed a few messages from Brittany and Nick, just the pleasantries.

"Gemma?" Brittany writes. "Are you there?"

Of course, I'm here. I'm always here. I'm always silent, but I'm always here.

"Couldn't drag me away from this meeting even if you tried," I write back.

"There she is," Nick writes.

I close my eyes again and breathe deeply. Why haven't I done this before? Staying in bed for work is so much better than getting out of bed.

"No!" Jack yells.

My eyes pop open. I guess there's no escaping Jack, not even in my comfortable bed.

"Yes!" Bill yells back. "We need that ASAP! It has to be this week."

Oh, how I've missed full-out shouting matches in the daily meeting. How did I ever survive without them?

It was bliss. It was peaceful bliss.

"There's no way!" Jack yells back.

"I missed that," Nick writes. "Can Jack do it or not?"

"I think it was a hell no," Brittany replies.

"All I'm saying is that I can't sign off on it unless it's tested by the end of the week," Bill yells.

"Did anyone else just mute the meeting? Because I did," Nick writes.

"Do they know that they don't have to yell?" Brittany asks.

"I don't think so," I write.

"Okay!" Carl finally breaks in. "Let's table this and move on."

"But I need it!" Bill says.

"I know! We will take it offline," Carl says.

"Hold up," Nick writes. "There is no offline anymore. Everything is online."

"Carl's new way of avoiding Bill," I reply.

"Took him long enough to stop the fight," Brittany says.

"He probably muted them, too," Nick says.

"Right, Gemma?" Carl says.

Shit. Shit. Shit. Do you even know what they are talking about?

I unmute myself, say, "Yes," and immediately mute myself again.

"I hate my life," I write in the chat.

"Cheer up," Brittany writes. "At least no one yelled at you."

"Give it time," Nick replies.

"Nick! No one yells at Gemma," Brittany responds.

"That's true. They'll be yelling at me."

"Nick," Carl says. "Have you finished that yet? It needs to be done this week."

Nick writes in the chat before answering, "See."

"No," he says out loud. "I was pulled off to work on a production defect. It won't be done this week."

"I need this done!" Bill yells.

Yeah. We get it. Calm down.

My heart speeds up and my head feels light. Just breathe. You are not in the same room as them. They can't see you. You can't see them. Just breathe.

I close my eyes and try to center myself as the yelling continues.

Just breathe. Don't even pay attention to the meeting. They don't need to talk to you at all. Just breathe.

"Okay, well that's it for the day. Talk to you all tomorrow," Carl says, and I see everyone's name hastily disappear from the participant list.

All right. Now immediately into my next meeting about web testing. It should be a fun one. I don't think I even have to be in this meeting. Why do I still go to meetings when I am not needed?

My name is the only one on the participants list. Where are they? Nick was literally just in my last meeting.

Maybe he had to make coffee. Or cry a little after the daily meeting.

Both fair explanations.

Nick's name appears. He says nothing and stays on mute. Fred's name appears. He says nothing and stays on mute, too. Bill's name appears, and he does the same.

Barbara's name shows up. "Morning everyone!" she says.

There are a few moments of silence. This is the time when everyone silently wonders who will be the nice coworker who unmutes themselves and says hi back. Sometimes, it is me. But it will certainly not be me for Barb.

Tick tock, people. Who will it be?

"Morning Barb," Nick mumbles.

And we have a winner.

I pull up a chat with Nick. "You are the loser this morning," I type.

"I am the loser every morning," he replies. "Don't you know that?"

"We are all losers every morning," I respond.

"Ain't that the truth."

"Okay!" Barb shouts. "Let's get this meeting started. Bill and Fred, why don't you get Nick and Gemma up to speed about what you are thinking for the testing process. That okay with everyone?"

"No," Nick writes to me. "That is not okay with me. I'd rather not do any of this work, especially for these three."

"I agree," I write back. "Not cool with me either."

"Nick? Gemma?" Barb inquires.

"Oh, shit," Nick writes. "Neither of us responded. It's your turn. I responded last time. You have the loser baton now."

"Ugh. Fine," I type back.

I unmute myself. "Yes, that works. Thanks, Barb."

"Thanks, Barb?" Nick types. "What the crap was that?"

"I don't know!" I respond. "I had the loser baton. I had to say something."

"You didn't have to thank her!"

I laugh out loud. "Okay! Well, that just means that you have to talk for both of us for the rest of the meeting."

"Okay, so if you have a question, just let me know, and I will be sure to say, Gemma wants to know this, but won't ask you herself."

I smile. "Totally fine with me," I write back.

"Damn it. You called my bluff. I would never."

"I know."

He responds with just a smiley face.

"So, are you paying attention?" I ask. "I have no idea what's going on."

"Partly. I am sure I can wing it."

"And that's what we were thinking," Bill says.

"Loser baton!" I quickly type to Nick.

"Sounds good," I hear Nick mumble.

"All right," Barb says. "Any more questions? I am sure, Nick, that you will need some time to see if you can make this happen."

Silence.

"She's talking to you!" I type to Nick.

"Right," Nick says out loud. "I will digest this and get back to you."

"Digest?" I write.

"Leave me alone! I wasn't even listening," he writes back.

"Great," Barb says. "I will set a follow-up meeting with all of us."

Oh, goodie.

Silence.

"Anything else for now?" Barb asks.

Silence.

As much as I love working from home, these crickets in virtual meetings somehow hit differently than in-person meetings.

"Okay, then talk to you all later," Barb says.

I see all three other names leave the meeting without saying goodbye.

Oh, shit. They left you holding the bag.

"Bye, Barb."

As I hit the leave meeting button, there is a knock on my door. I don't move. I only turn my head to look at the door and then down to look at the leggings and over-sized T-shirt I am wearing.

"It's me," I hear Walter say through the door. "I brought coffee."

Music to my ears.

Not giving my outfit another thought or even smoothing out my hair, I get up and let him in.

"Morning, kid," he says. "I brought you a coffee from Sally's. I hope you're not in the middle of a meeting."

What a guy.

"Thank you. We just ended the meeting right before you knocked. It was perfect timing. Come in."

Walter walks over to the couch, and I pick up my laptop from the bed, place it onto the coffee table so I can see the screen, and sit down next to him.

"I don't want to bother you if you have to work."

"Don't worry about it. As long as my computer doesn't go to sleep, I'm fine. To everyone else, it will still look like I am working."

I wink at Walter, and he smiles. Taking sip of coffee, I lean back against the couch and cross my legs.

"Where's Josh this morning?" I ask.

"He was up late working. He was on the phone and computer all night. Kid doesn't know how to take a vacation. Anyway, I'm letting him sleep in."

"How was Sally this morning?"

"Good. Good. She's definitely closing up early now. She changed the sign and everything. She says she likes the new hours. I don't blame her. She was working long days without a break. It's good for her to finally take some time for herself."

"I know. I'm going to miss her casserole, though."

"Me too, kid. I will just have to invite her over for dinner again and ask her to bring it."

"Sounds like a plan. I had a lot of fun last night. I'm glad you invited Sally."

"Yeah, it was fun. Josh said he enjoyed meeting both of you. I talk about you two a lot."

I lean over, move my cursor, and then rest back against the couch, again.

"You know…" I start.

"Yeah?"

"He said that I remind him of his mother."

"Yes." Walter brings his hand up to his head and scratches behind his ear. "She was touched by the sadness, as well."

We both sit silently for a few minutes and sip our coffee.

That explains it. That explains why he is so understanding and accepting of me, even in my worst moods. I always knew he understood. Because he does.

"She was also a charmer, just like you, with a keen wit."

Charmer? Me?

"I don't know about those."

"Well, I do."

Looking at me from the side of his eye, he grins. He then gives my apartment a once over and frowns.

"This is small," he says. "Too small."

"I know, but it's all I can afford in this building. And I like being so close to work. And you." I wink.

"You like this working from home business?"

"Yeah, I do."

Looking down at my outfit, he waves his finger in the air. "You're in your pajamas, and you haven't brushed your hair. And you're cooped up in this small place."

"It's not as bad as it seems. I've never been able to wear pajamas during the day at work, so this is pretty awesome for me."

"I can see that, I guess. But you don't leave your apartment or see anyone. You still see that Nate of yours?"

"Yeah. Not as much since we're not in the office, and he's in San Francisco right now. But, yes."

"I like him."

"I do, too."

"He's good for you. I can see myself in him. He's good people."

I lean over once again and move my cursor.

"Well, I don't want to intrude."

"You could never."

I take another sip of coffee.

"Josh didn't just come out for a visit," Walter says.

"No?"

"He's been trying to get me to move out to New York ever since his mother passed."

What? No! Not Walter. He can't take Walter.

"Are you going to?" I ask.

"I don't want to. But I am probably going to have to eventually."

"I don't want you to."

"I know. But he wants me closer in case anything happens. It would be nice to see him and Julia more often, especially for holidays."

No. I can feel him starting to consider moving. No, he can't leave. I won't let him.

"I would miss you so much," I say.

"I would miss you too. So, I guess you'll have to move to New York with me," he says and smiles.

CHAPTER THIRTEEN

"Why do you think you haven't talked to him yet?" Stacey asks.

Why do I come here? She makes me talk about my feelings.

"I don't know."

"Do you think you are scared of what he'll say?"

"Maybe."

"Do you think that he's scared of what *you* might say? You did stop talking to him for a week or two."

"I hadn't considered that."

"Is he back yet?"

"No. He'll be back on Sunday."

She's going to make me see him, isn't she?

"Are you going to see him?"

Damn it.

"I don't know. It depends how he feels, I guess. He will just have flown back after a week away, and he'll have to work the next day."

"Are you trying to be considerate of his feelings or trying to come up with an excuse not to see him?"

Burn. That was harsh.

"Maybe both."

"Why do you think that is?"

Why does she always have to ask me that? Can't she just tell me what she thinks?

"I don't want to fight again and..."

And Nick. Tell her about Nick.

"And?"

"And there's...I'm not sure what it is. I shouldn't even talk about it."

"That's why we're here, Gemma. To talk about things, especially things you don't want to talk about."

I know, and I hate it.

"It's just my coworker. We've been getting kind of closer, and I feel really comfortable with him, and he makes me laugh."

"You have feelings for this person?"

"No. I mean, I don't think so."

"What else can you tell me about this coworker?"

"His name is Nick. I've known him for a few years. He is who Nate would call my work husband."

"I see. You've talked to Nate about him?"

"Yes. Another thing that Nate was mad about. He was upset that I always talked about Nick, which I don't, and that I let Nick save me."

"Save you?"

"Yeah. I set up my meeting with Nick right after my meeting with Jack so that Nick could barge in if we went over time."

Stacey laughs. "I see. What else have you told Nate about Nick?"

"Nothing. Just that we had fun at the work party at Fenway Park. But Brittany was with us. Brittany is always with us."

"Nate is jealous of Nick?"

"Apparently."

"And does he have reason to be?"

Does he? Why are we even talking about Nick anyway? He is just a coworker.

"Nothing has happened. I'm not sure I want anything to. I guess I'm just confused. I get along so well with Nick."

"And you don't with Nate?"

"Not lately."

"Do you think you'd be thinking about Nick this way if things were good with Nate?"

"I'm not sure."

"Is it possible that you are only wondering about Nick because things are so up in the air with Nate right now?"

"It's possible."

"You did say you weren't sure about your feelings for Nick."

"True."

"Are you still worried about Nate wanting to control the relationship or you?"

"I'm a little worried. I don't know how I feel about it."

"Do you ever feel controlled by him?"

"No."

"You have said in the past that he calms your anxiety when you're around him."

"Yes. He is a calming presence. Or he was."

"Do you think it's possible that you actually like that he takes control? There is less anxiety for you that way. You don't feel as out of control yourself."

Well, shit. This is why I pay her the big bucks, I guess. I never thought of that.

"That never crossed my mind."

"Do you think that it is accurate?"

Shit, yes.

"Yes. That actually makes a lot of sense. He brings a calm and an order to my life. He calms me down. I never thought about him being in control as a good thing, but it does actually help me."

"Maybe it not only calms your anxiety, but also calms his own. So, maybe it's not such a bad thing, after all?"

"Maybe not."

"You also said that you were worried that he doesn't understand you and your anxiety."

"Yes."

"If it is underlying anxiety causing his need for control, he may just be able to relate to you after all."

"I guess so."

"Do you feel better about talking to him now?"

"Yes."

164

"Will you talk to him when he gets back?"

Damn it. I knew that was coming, eventually.

"I suppose."

"Good. Are you still working from home?"

"Yes."

"Any news on when the office might reopen?"

I sigh. "Maybe a week, if that."

"Have you thought about asking your boss if you could permanently work from home?"

Say what? For real? I can do that?

"Is that an option?"

"It's only an option if you ask."

"I don't think he'll let me, at least, not every day."

"That's a start. Not every day is not every day. You won't have five days in the office."

"True."

"Just think about it. You don't have to bring it up to him if you don't want to."

Damn right, I'll think about it. I will pray, just like I prayed for the building to shut down.

I leave Stacey's office on a slightly hopeful note, get into a Road Trip, and flop back down onto my couch. Is it even possible that I could work from home after the building is reopened?

Maybe. But you wouldn't see anyone anymore.

So?

What about Brittany? And Nick?

They will deal. Besides, we are going out on Friday.

What about McGruff?

I don't know. I wonder what he is doing right now.

You should call him.

What? No.

He would be happy to hear from you.

Would he, though?

Yes. He would. Just do it.

Picking up my phone, I look at my reflection and smooth out my hair. I press the video chat button and stare at my face while it says connecting.

He's not going to pick up.

Give him a minute to answer.

It's taking too long. He's not going to answer. He's avoiding me.

My phone blips and then disconnects.

He didn't answer.

There's no reason to get upset. He is probably busy at a presentation or something.

I toss my phone onto the coffee table and flop down face first onto the couch.

He doesn't want to talk to me.

Seriously? He's at a conference. He's busy. Don't get all emotional.

I close my eyes for a moment and breathe deeply. In and out. In and out. My mind clears for a microsecond before my phone starts to buzz, and my eyes flip open. I bounce up to a sitting position and grab my phone.

It's him.

Well, answer it.

Should I?

Yes! You were just pouting that he didn't answer your call. Now answer it!

I do, and his beautiful face appears on my phone. His eyes light up.

"Hey, there. Did I wake you up?" he asks.

I quickly glance at my own face. My hair is a mess. Hurriedly, I run my hands over my head.

"No."

He smiles his adorable smile.

"Sorry I missed your call. I was just finishing up in a presentation about new testing software. I think you would have liked it. It was pretty cool. I will have to show you their stuff when I get back."

"Yeah. I'd like to see it."

His eyes sparkle. "Good."

"How's it going over there?"

"I know I'm going to sound like a nerd when I say this, but it's actually been really fun."

"Oh, my God. Nerd!"

"I know. I'm learning a lot, and the guys I've met here are really nice. This one guy, Rafael, he's from Arizona, and after talking for a few minutes, we realized we both went to Northeastern University. How crazy is that? We even had a class together."

"That's so weird."

"Enough about me. Tell me about you."

"Not much to report back on here."

"Has Walter asked you to go to tai chi, again?"

"No. Thank goodness. I'm not ready to show my face there again quite so soon. Oh, my God! I forgot! I had dinner with Walter and Josh."

"What? How did you forget that? That's like breaking news."

"I know. I'm such a dummy."

"Tell me about it."

"What? Are you agreeing that I am a dummy?"

McGruff smiles. "No, dummy. I was asking you to tell me about the dinner with Walter and his son."

I try not to smile. "Well, his name is Josh, according to Walter, but he calls himself Joshua. So, obviously, I was weird and awkward about saying his name."

"Obviously." He smiles.

Do everyone's eyes sparkle like McGruff's?

"Oh! And Sally was there."

"Sally! Out of the coffee shop? I didn't think she existed elsewhere."

"I know! It was amazing."

"So, you had fun?"

"Yeah. But Sally did tell us that she is closing at two o'clock now. No more dinner for us."

"Don't worry. I'll feed you."

I smile. "That's exactly what Walter said."

"We just want to take care of our girl."

My heart flutters.

Stop that right this instant.

"The building is still closed," I say.

"I heard. How is working from home going?"

"I love it so much. It's so much less stressful. I can work in my pajamas."

"Oh, yeah? Are you wearing your pjs now?"

"Maybe…"

"Do they have little sheep on them?"

"Of course. Don't all respectable pjs?"

"Mine do, obviously."

"Did you take them with you to San Francisco?"

"Of course, I did. I sit on my balcony in the morning sipping coffee in my sheepy pjs."

"So do I. Minus the balcony."

"Coffee?"

"Yep. I started drinking it again while I'm at home."

"What! You said you had nothing to report, and then I hear about Walter and Sally and Josh, and now you are drinking coffee again?"

"Yep, the dynamic duo is back together. Not for long, though. I will probably stop again when we go back to the office. But this is like a cheat week or weeks. It doesn't count."

"No wonder you look so happy. It suits you."

I stare into his eyes for a moment and then look down. My heart beats faster.

"When will you be back?"

"My flight is Sunday morning."

"Do you have to work on Monday?"

"Yep. No rest for the weary."

"You mean wicked."

"Yes, I do." A devilish grin appears on his face. "Tell me more about dinner with Josh."

"Well, I drank too much wine."

"Of course. Was it awkward silence like you thought it would be?"

"No. Sally was there, remember?"

"Oh, right. So, you aren't scared of Josh anymore?"

"Oh, I am definitely scared of him, but not as much as before."

McGruff smiles.

"But he is trying to get Walter to move to New York with him," I add.

"What? No!"

"My thoughts exactly. But Walter said I could move to NYC with him when he goes." I smile.

"Not without me, you don't. There's no way I am staying here without Walter."

"Just Walter?"

"Yeah, what else would it be?"

The corner of his mouth curves up.

CHAPTER FOURTEEN

What the heck am I doing? Why am I in the backseat of this Ford Focus heading to Somerville to hang out with Brittany and Nick?

Because you like them?

I suppose. But more importantly, why have I voluntarily left my apartment?

It will be good for you. You don't see human beings much anymore.

Seeing other humans is overrated.

Thankfully, Brittany is here before me and has claimed a table. She waves me over when she sees me.

"Hey! You made it!" she says.

Yep. Here I am.

It is a square table with four seats. I take a seat next to her, or rather diagonal to her. The pub is not yet crowded, but there are quite a few other people here right after work; the bar seating is at full capacity. There are only tables, no booths, and the lights are dim, so I can barely make out anyone's face beyond Brittany's.

"Been waiting long?" I ask.

"Nope. Just got here."

"Have you heard from Nick? Is he still coming?"

Please say no. Please say no.

"Yep. He's on his way."

Why don't you want to see Nick?

No reason. I would just rather spend time with Brittany.

Right.

But he does show up. He arrives a few minutes later wearing khakis and a polo shirt.

"Why are you so fancy?" Brittany asks.

"Don't get out much anymore," he responds. "Plus, I need to look good for my two favorite ladies."

"Oh, please," Brittany says.

Nick pulls out a chair and then stops. "Have you guys ordered yet?"

"No, it's bar service."

"Okay, I'll go get us some beers."

"Thanks, Nick," I say.

"How is everything?" Brittany asks me as Nick walks away.

"It is fine. How are you?"

"Fine. Are you still feeling like you need a new job?"

"Always. But I won't. I actually do like my job and the company."

"I know. But if you do leave, you know that you have to take me with you, right?"

I laugh. "Yes, I know. And I will."

"Good. Just don't tell Nick."

"Tell me what?" Nick asks as he places the beers on the table.

"Oh, nothing," Brittany says. "Just girl stuff."

"Yuck," he responds.

"That's right," I say, "Yuck."

"So," Nick starts, "tell me what your home offices look like and what you are wearing to work these days."

"That's a little personal," Brittany answers.

"Whoa. Okay, so…undies?"

"No!" Brittany shouts. "It's not like that. I just haven't really been dressing up as much as I usually do for work."

"Neither have I," I add. "I'm mostly in leggings and T-shirts these days."

"Okay, good," Nick says. "I was joking, but honestly, I wear the same thing every single day now. I don't even care."

"Oh, thank God," Brittany says. "Me too."

"Where is your setup?" Nick asks. "I am at my kitchen table."

"Same," Brittany responds.

They both look at me.

I hate when they do that. Why can't I just be a silent observer?

"Well, I switch back and forth between my couch and coffee table and my breakfast bar. I'm not cool enough to have an actual kitchen table."

Sometimes, you work in bed, too.

They don't have to know that. I already told them I'm in basically pajamas. They don't have to wonder if I'm in bed when we have meetings together or if I'm wrapped up in a blanket like a papoose waiting for the meeting to be over so that I can curl up on the couch. They don't need to know that.

"I remember," Nick says. "Your apartment is tiny."

"At least, I don't have a deer head on my wall!"

"Hey! You said you liked it."

"Whoa," Brittany interjects. "You've been to each other's apartments?"

"No," I say. "I accidentally made us have a video meeting because I didn't know that everyone was just doing voice."

"That was the day the crane collapsed," Nick says. "We were in the meeting when everything just went dead."

The day my dreams came true.

"Do you guys like it?" Brittany asks. "Working from home, that is."

"I do. It's much more relaxed," Nick says.

They both look at me. Again.

"I adore it," I say.

"Me too," Brittany replies.

"I don't know what I'm going to do when they make us go back," I say.

"We should protest," Nick says. "Have a sit in or something."

"A sit in?" I ask. "We would have to actually *go in* for that. And I don't ever want to go back."

"Valid point," he replies.

"How about we all just go on strike?" Brittany adds.

"That could work," Nick says. "We would just have to get most of our coworkers to join us."

"I am sure most would," Brittany replies.

"Not Jack," I say. "Or Barb."

"Screw them!" Nick says.

"I wouldn't mind if I never saw them again," I say.

"Jack and Barb?" Brittany asks.

Or any of them.

"For starters," I say.

"Well, you would obviously see us," she responds.

"Obviously," I say. "I'm here, aren't I?"

"Even though I practically had to beg you."

Lies.

"This is a cool place," I say to change the subject. "Do you come here often?"

"Are you hitting on Brittany?" Nick asks.

"What if I am?"

"I just thought you had a guy you were sort of seeing."

"She does," Brittany answers.

"Ah," he says. "Do you two want another drink?"

"Sure!" Brittany answers.

They both look at me.

Can I say no? If I do, will I have to sit here sober? Can I call a Road Trip without them knowing? I will just go to the bathroom and never come back. I am sure McGruff would approve of that move in this situation. He will feel better that I do it to other people too.

"Gemma?" Nick asks.

"Sure."

Damn it. Why did you say yes? You could be on your way home by now.

Nick gets up to walk to the bar. I watch him walk away before I lean over to Brittany and quietly ask, "Do you and Nick have a thing?"

"A thing?"

"Yes, a thing."

"No. We don't."

"Are you sure? Do you want a thing?"

"Honestly, I haven't thought about it because he is so into you."

"Me?"

"Yes, it's so obvious."

"I don't think so. Are you sure he's not into you? He seems like he is to me."

"No. It's okay, Gemma."

"No, but…"

"Gem, McGruff followed you around for weeks, and you didn't believe he liked you."

Low blow, Brittany. Low blow.

"Okay, but Nick knows about McGruff."

Brittany just shrugs.

"Besides," I say, "you two are so cute together. You would be better with him than me."

"Don't get weird. I didn't mean anything by it. I'm sorry that I said anything."

Don't get weird? Weird's my MO.

"No, it's okay. You know I get awkward."

Brittany laughs. "So how is McGruff, anyway? You haven't talked about him much. But it is weird lately since we haven't really seen each other at all."

"Yeah. He's been in San Francisco all week at a conference. He is flying back Sunday. But now that you mention it…"

"Yes? Mention what?"

"McGruff has gotten a little jealous of Nick lately. Maybe I shouldn't have come out tonight."

"Jealous of Nick? You are so into McGruff though."

"I know! I've tried to tell him that, but apparently I talk about Nick a lot. That's only because I had to have meetings with him. And then the three of us hung out at Fenway and went out after. So, maybe I can see why he's a little jealous."

"Gem, I know you are completely captivated by McGruff. He will see it, too."

"Yeah."

But am I? Am I still completely captivated by McGruff?

"Don't let it get to you, Gemma. Nick knows you are seeing someone. It's not like you have feelings for Nick, right?"

"Right."

Of course, right. It's not like I chat with him about nothing and everything during our meetings. It's not like I feel comfortable with him. It's not like we laugh together all the time. No, of course, I don't have feelings for Nick. I am completely captivated by McGruff.

Nick reappears and places a beer bottle in front of each of us.

"Thanks," Brittany says.

Act normal. Just act normal. Do not be weird. Do not do or say anything weird.

"Yeah, thanks, Nicholas," I say.

What the hell was that? I said don't be weird! And you go and be weird!

"Nicholas?" Nick questions.

Out of the corner of my eye, I see Brittany grinning at me.

"Yeah, we were just talking about how your proper name is actually pretty cool," Brittany says.

Thank God for Brittany. She saves me in and out of work.

Don't let McGruff hear you say that someone else is now allowed to save you, too.

Oh, shut up.

"I guess it is pretty cool," he says.

Oh, my God, Gemma. Can you just be normal for once?

No. The answer to that is no.

175

Gem of Uncertainty

For the remainder of the evening, I try to avoid eye contact with Nick completely. And I deploy my only defense in this situation, which is to guzzle my beer.

Calm down. Why did Brittany have to tell me that Nick is into me? Now, look at me. I am a quivering mess when I am usually fine around Nick. This is just stupid.

"Another round?" Nick asks.

"No!" I respond quickly.

They both look at me.

"I am not feeling well, so I should be going," I say.

"Oh no," Brittany says. "I should be going too, though."

"Ah, well. The ladies are always running out on me. Let me just take care of the check."

"No! Not this time!" Brittany says.

"Too late!" Nick says and hurries towards the bar.

"Are you okay?" Brittany asks me.

"No. I am an anxious freak. You shouldn't have told me that about Nick. It messed me right up."

"I'm sorry. I should have thought about that before I spoke."

"You did save me with the whole Nicholas thing, though, so thank you."

"I couldn't leave a girl hanging, especially when it was my fault."

"All right," Nick says, as he approaches the table. "You two ready?"

"I'll meet you guys outside. I just need to run to the restroom," Brittany says and walks towards the back wall of the pub.

What? No? She cannot leave me. She cannot leave me alone with Nick.

"After you," Nick says.

I smile awkwardly and walk out the door with Nick trailing behind me. We stand next to each other on the curb.

Please let my car get here first.

Hush. You're fine. Nothing weird is going to happen. Just forget what Brittany said.

My heart starts to pound. Why is my heart pounding? This is stupid. Calm down. My breath quickens, and my head feels light. Stop this. Stop this right now. It is just Nick. You are dating McGruff. And he knows it.

I can feel him staring at me. Oh, goodness. Where is my car? Can I walk home from here? It's only like, what, eight miles? That is totally doable. No. I will just reroute my Road Trip. Yeah, that's a much better idea. Okay. I should start walking now before anything...

"Gemma..."

Oh, no. I waited too long.

Taking a deep breath, I turn to look at him. His eyes are large and bright. His lips are slightly parted.

"Yeah?" I say softly.

"You...I..."

Nope. It's happening again. Just start walking. That's not rude at all. Just go.

But I don't. I just stand there staring into his eyes, his big, watery eyes.

Leave, Gemma. Leave.

But I don't. I stand there watching him search for the right words to say and failing to find them. I just stand there watching his eyes watch mine.

"I...you..."

He's not going to say it. Thank goodness. He's not going to say it. I don't think he will.

Turn and run, Gemma. Turn and run.

But I don't. I just stand there as he inches closer and closer to me. I just stand there as his eyes flick from my eyes down to my lips and then back to my eyes. I just stand there as his hand slowly reaches for my face.

"Hey!" Brittany comes bursting out of the pub. "Sorry, there was a line."

Nick and I both take a giant step back as Brittany walks up and stands between us on the curb.

Please let my car get here first. Please let my car get here first.

And it does. My prayers are answered when a green Camry stops in front of us. I quickly step forward, open the door, call over my shoulder, "Bye. See you, I mean, talk to you Monday," get in, and slam the door shut before they can even respond. As the car drives away, I rest my forehead on the back of the passenger side seat.

"Rough night?" the driver asks.

Oh my God, yes. I need to talk to Liz about this.

I stay up tossing and turning about how dumb it was for me to just stand there while Nick walked up to me like that. What was I thinking? Did I even want to kiss him?

Yes.

No.

Maybe.

Of course, you didn't. You are dating McGruff.

Then why didn't I run away? Why did I just stand there?

You are weird and don't do normal things.

Thank goodness Liz does not cancel on me. Getting out of my Road Trip, I close the door to the car and step onto the curb in front of Flannery's.

How do you get yourself into these things?

Nothing has happened. There is no thing.

Not yet, anyway.

I open the door to the bar, scan the chairs, and walk over and sit next to Liz. Before she even says anything, I put my elbows on the bar and hide my face in my hands. Greg places a drink down in front of me.

"What is up with you today?" she asks me.

"There's this guy," I say.

178

"Whoa!" Liz exclaims.

"It's not like that."

"It's always like that. Right, Greg?"

Greg is leaning over the bar in front of us.

"Yes. He likes you," Greg says.

"I haven't even said anything! I could say he ran over my cat."

"You have a cat?" Greg asks.

"No. That's not the point."

"No story has ever started with 'There's this guy,' and went on to say, 'He ran over my cat,'" Greg says.

"I guess that's true," I say.

Greg raises an eyebrow. "What happened to the other guy? The one that used to come in here?"

"Nothing. We are still dating."

"Then why are you starting a story with 'There's this guy?'" Greg asks.

Yeah, Gemma, why are you?

"Never mind. I don't have anything to talk about. There is no guy."

"Mhmm," Greg says.

"Greg," Liz interjects, "could we please get some girl time, here?"

"I thought that's what we were doing?"

"I mean, just the two of us. Gemma and me."

"Oh." Greg pouts and walks off.

"So, do tell," Liz says.

"I told you. It's not like that. Stacey thinks that I am only thinking about him because things with Nate are so up in the air right now."

"You talked to Stacey about him before you talked to me?"

"There's nothing to talk about."

"Clearly, there is if you brought him up to Stacey, and you were going to bring him up now."

She's got you there.

"Start at the beginning," Liz says. "Who is this guy?"

"Nick."

"Your coworker?"

"Yes."

"Did something happen between you two?"

"No."

There was that moment last night.

Do not call it a moment.

"You have feelings for him?"

"No! I mean, I don't know."

Liz scrunches up her face. "Okay, so what is going on with him, then?"

I take a deep breath. "As I said, nothing, but Brittany mentioned last night that she thought he was into me. That's all."

"Last night?"

"Yeah, I met her and Nick for a drink."

"You went out with Nick last night?"

"And Brittany. We were never alone."

Except for that one moment.

"Did you want to be alone?"

"No. Besides, I have Nate."

"I know. I like Nate. I do. But I like you more. And I want you to be happy, and if that's not going to be with Nate, then that's okay. I'm on your side. Always."

"Me too!" Greg shouts over to us.

"Greg!" Liz reprimands, and he turns around. "So?" she asks me.

"I know. But this is nothing. I'm with Nate. I want to be with Nate."

"If this is nothing, then why even bring it up? Why talk to Stacey about him?"

You walked right back into that one.

I sigh. "I guess you're right."

"So, tell me about him."

"We've been talking a lot more, lately. Carl made me set up meetings with him, as I've told you before." Liz nods. "And I had to go back to the daily meeting, and he is in there. Brittany and he have become friends, so they are inviting me to hang out with them, and we are always talking during the daily meeting now since it is virtual."

"So, you like him?"

"I enjoy talking to him. He's funny and makes me laugh, and I feel comfortable around him."

"And nothing has happened?"

"No. Well, there may have been a moment last night."

"Okay. That's something, I guess. Do you want something to happen?"

"I don't know. Things have been so crazy with Nate, and we have been fighting. I just haven't been feeling like I had about him."

"Do you not like him because you're not feeling well, or do you just not like him anymore?"

"I don't know."

"Have you talked to Nate about any of this?"

"Not really. I was avoiding him, and then he was in San Francisco."

"He's coming home this weekend, right?"

"Yes. He should be home tomorrow."

"Good. I really think you should talk to him about how you are feeling."

"I know I should."

"What are you going to do about Nick?"

"Nothing. I'm not even sure how I feel about him."

"Are you going to talk to him again?"

"I have to. I have to talk to him about work almost every day."

Standing a few feet away, Greg asks, "Is it safe to come back now?"

Liz looks at me, and I nod. "Yes," she says.

"Okay, good. I know you don't want me to, but I'm going to give you my two cents."

"You're right. We don't want you to," Liz jokes.

Greg side eyes her but continues to talk to me. "I have known you for a while now, Gemma, and I must say, that you have never looked happier than with Nate. That's all I'm going to say."

Liz looks at me. "He's kind of right."

"Of course, I am. Plus, he does seem to like you a lot. And he's pretty good looking. For a guy."

Maybe they are right. McGruff does make you happy, doesn't he?

He used to. I'm not sure anymore.

But you did have side effects from your medication. Maybe when you see him again, you'll feel better since you've stopped taking Zoloft.

Maybe.

"Okay, so you two are Team Nate, then?" I ask.

"I don't know about that," Greg says. "I haven't met the other guy. He needs to come here so I can check him out."

"Check him out!" Liz shouts.

"You know what I mean."

CHAPTER FIFTEEN

I open my calendar to look at the day's meetings. There's the morning shitshow, a follow-up with the QA team for web testing, and my monthly meeting with Carl.

Damn it. Nick is in the QA meeting.

Other people are in there, too. He won't be able to talk to you about Friday. It'll be fine.

And my monthly meeting with Carl? Didn't I just have that?

Yeah, a month ago.

Well, it feels like it was last week. What if I just didn't log on to the meetings?

Any of them?

Yep. I can say my Wi-Fi went out.

All day?

Okay, what if I call in sick? I haven't been sick in ages. How does one call in sick nowadays when we are all at home anyway?

With your luck, they would just reschedule the meetings. The daily meeting, they won't cancel, but it will reappear tomorrow; there's no avoiding it. It will come for you. Carl will definitely reschedule your monthly meeting. And QA...yeah, that's a wildcard. They may have it without you.

Okay. I will take that. I should absolutely call in sick today to avoid meetings and life and conversations and just lie in bed all day.

But I don't. I log into the daily meeting just like I always do, and I am the first one in cyberspace, just like I always am. And of course, Nick is the first name to pop up on the participants list.

No. Nope. Someone else, please log on. I cannot be alone in cyberspace with him. I don't want him to talk to me.

But he doesn't. He stays on mute until every other name is added to the participant list.

What? Does he not want to talk to me?

You were just praying that he didn't talk to you. Now you want him to?

No. I just don't want him to not want to talk to me.

What does that even mean?

I don't want him to be mad at me.

Why would he be mad at you?

I don't know. Maybe because I just awkwardly ran away from him on Friday night and haven't talked to him since?

"Right, Gemma?" Carl asks.

Shit. Shitty McShit Shit. Why can I never pay attention ever? I didn't even realize the meeting had started.

"Yep," I say out loud.

There is a conspicuous lack of talking in the chat group this morning. No one has said anything. Is Brittany mad at me, too?

Too? You don't know that Nick is mad at you.

I open a chat message with only Brittany.

"Happy Monday?" I type.

"Why is the weekend so short?" she responds.

Okay. She's not mad.

"It's a cruel world," I reply.

"That it is."

"Have you talked to Nick? He's quiet this morning."

"No. He seemed really weird after you took off on Friday. He didn't even talk to me while we waited. It was odd."

Okay. So, this *is* all my fault, and he is mad.

You should tell her.

No. There's nothing to tell. Plus, it'd be weird.

"Did he say anything to you?" she asks.

Damn it. Now I have to tell her.

"Nick, can you take care of that?" Carl asks.

"Yes. I will have it done by the end of the day."

"He speaks," Brittany writes.

"And he's paying attention," I respond.

Great. Maybe she will forget her question.

"So?" she writes. "Did he talk to you?"

Damn her.

"Yeah…I think you were right."

"About what?"

"Him having a thing for me."

"I knew it! What happened?"

"Technically nothing. But things did get weird for a second."

"And then I came out, and you ran away."

"Yep."

"That explains it then."

Unfortunately. I messed it all up. Things were finally good, and I messed it up.

"Okay, that is it for today," I hear Carl say. "I will give you twenty minutes back."

I watch as all of the names disappear from the participant list.

Why do you do this to yourself? You had a great thing going with McGruff, and you screwed it up. You had a good friendship going with Nick, and you screwed that up too.

I don't know. It's just what I do.

Well, stop it.

I watch the clock slowly move forward until it is time for the QA meeting with Nick.

Son of a bitch. Can I just not log on for this? Do they even need me?

Probably not. But you should log on anyway. Just stay muted the whole time.

I am the first to log on. I wait in silence for Fred, Bill, Barb, and Nick to all log on. And yes, they do not actually need me. I don't even know why I go to meetings; I am never actually needed.

"Thanks, everyone," Barb says, and her name drops from the list.

"Okay, well I will talk to you later," Bill says.

"Bye, guys," Fred says and drops off.

"Gemma," Nick says quickly. "Would you mind hanging on for a second?"

Yes. I would mind. I would absolutely mind. It is almost lunchtime, and my stomach will not make it through one more minute without food. And I object to being left alone with you.

"Sure."

Why did you just say sure?

What was I supposed to say, no?

Yes! You should have said no. You should have said hell no and then left the meeting, disconnected from work, given Carl your resignation, and then moved to Thailand. That's what you should have done.

Everyone else has signed off, and the two of us are left alone in silence.

"Would you," he starts, "would you mind going on video for a minute?"

What? Yes, I would mind. I would absolutely mind. I look like absolute trash, and I'd rather never see him in person or on video ever again.

"Sure."

Why did you just say sure? Have you not looked in the mirror today? Oh, wait. No, you haven't. You look like garbage.

What was I supposed to say, no?

Yes! You should have said no. You are terribly sorry, but you have come down with a bad case of amnesia, and you don't remember who he is, and you don't remember who you are, so you are going to the hospital now and will hopefully live out the rest of your days on a beach in Hawaii, never remembering any of this madness that you call a job or a life.

"So…" he begins.

No. Nope. Sign off now. Sign off now.

But I don't. After he turns on his video so that I can see his face and his big vulnerable eyes, I click the video button on the meeting and broadcast my own face to him.

"Hey," he says when he sees my face. His eyes light up, and the corner of his mouth curves up. His hair is combed, and he is clean shaven. He looks good, much better than I do.

"I just wanted to talk about Friday night."

"Nick, we are working. This is a work meeting."

"I know. But I wasn't sure how else to talk to you."

"By phone?"

"Yeah. I guess now that I think about it, that would have been less weird."

"Yeah…"

"Anyway, I like you, Gemma."

"Nick, I'm dating someone."

Whoa. Hard shut down.

"I know. But I had to put it out there that I would like to take you out. Do you want to go out with me? Just me? You don't have to answer now. You can think about it. But I think we'd be really good together."

Please, don't let this be happening.

Oh, this is happening all right.

"Nick…"

There is a knock on my door. Who the heck could that be? Walter?

"There is someone at my door," I say. "I'll be right back."

I watch him sigh and look down.

Why did you do this to him?

What did I do to him? He did this to himself.

I quickly open the door, expecting Walter, only to find the beautiful McGruff standing nonchalantly across the doorway.

What? Why?

He looks up and smiles. "Hey," he smoothly says.

187

"Hey," I awkwardly say.

"I'm sorry if I am interrupting. I just wanted to see you since I got in too late last night to even call."

"No, no. Not interrupting anything. At all."

Smooth. Real smooth.

"You're not working?"

"Oh, yeah, just work."

"Can I come in?"

Shit, Gemma.

"Yes! Of course."

My eyes follow him as he walks over to the breakfast bar. I close the door and walk straight to my computer. Leaning over my laptop, I move the mouse and hover the cursor over the leave meeting button.

"Sorry, I have to go."

"Now?"

"Yes, sorry."

"Okay. But think about what I said."

"Okay."

I click the leave button and turn to face McGruff.

"Was that Nick?"

"Yes. We work together."

Well, that was bitchier than I wanted.

McGruff sighs. "I know. I'm sorry I got so upset about him. I don't get mad when you talk about Brittany. I shouldn't get mad when you talk about Nick."

Shouldn't he though? At least, now he has a reason to be mad. Not that he knows that Nick literally just asked me out probably while he was outside my door.

Shut up this instant.

"Are you not working today?" I ask.

"My boss gave me a half day because I got in so late last night. He thinks I'm napping."

"Well, I still have to work today."

"I know. But I was hoping you would have lunch with me." He holds up a brown paper bag. "I got lunch from Sally's."

You can't say no to a free lunch.

Can't I?

He's already here and so is the food.

"I didn't mean for you to end your meeting. I would have waited for you to finish."

Oh, yeah. That would have been great. Have McGruff listen in on Nick asking me out. What could possibly go wrong with that? McGruff is already paranoid about him.

And apparently, he should be?

"Yeah, of course, we can have lunch together. I'd never pass up a Sally's lunch. Sit down." I motion towards the breakfast bar, and McGruff sets down the bag and pulls out a chair.

"Turkey and cheese?" I ask.

He smiles wryly. "But of course."

I slide into the seat next to him and take a bite of the sandwich.

"How's work going?" he asks.

"It's fine. Nothing out of the ordinary."

Way to be sketchy. There is so something out of the ordinary.

"And your weekend?" he follows with.

What the crap? What does he know?

Probably nothing. He's just chatting with you.

"It was okay. How was your flight?"

"Got delayed for a while, but other than that, it got me back home."

"Yep. It did."

"Did you see Liz this weekend?"

Damn it. Can't he just drop it?

"Yes."

Tell him. Tell him about Friday.

"And I went out with Brittany and Nick on Friday."

"I see."

Oh, crap. Here it comes.

"Look, Gemma. I don't want to be this guy. I don't want to be the guy that gets jealous of other guys that you talk to. And I definitely don't want to control you. I'm sorry that I ever said that. I don't want to. I've never wanted to. You are, in fact, uncontrollable."

"I kind of wish I were controllable."

"Don't say that. Never say that. You are perfect just as you are. I wouldn't change a thing."

"I'd change lots of things."

"Well, I wouldn't."

"So, will you tell me why you feel like you are not in control around me? Or why you feel the need to always be in control?"

"The first question is easy. It's because I like you so much. I feel like everything I do or say pushes you away. I know that's not your fault. It's mine. I'm sorry if I made you feel otherwise. I was a jerk."

"It's okay. But everything you do doesn't push me away. That's just how I react to things. I run away."

"I am finally understanding that. And your second question is not as easy. See, my dad was a military man. I never felt like anything I did was good enough for him, so I had to have everything perfect. I had to have control over everything."

My eyes glaze over, and I stare blankly.

"Gemma? Did I say something?"

"Yes. You did. You said you are a perfectionist, and I am, too. My anxiety just comes out as physical and emotional anxiety. Yours comes out as a need for control. I absolutely get it."

He is silent for a moment. "You know, I never thought about it as anxiety, but that is absolutely what it is. You're right. I guess we have more in common than I thought."

"It's just another side of the coin. I wanted to talk to you so much about my anxiety and the medication I am on, but I didn't know how you would react."

"Gemma, you can tell me anything. I would never judge you, especially about that."

"Okay…"

"You said you're on medication?"

"Yes. And it was making me irritable and cranky and tired and sweaty, and I didn't know how to explain that to you."

His face softens. "Just like that would have been fine. I'm sorry, I should have seen that you were going through something."

"No. I should have told you."

"So, are we okay?"

"Yeah, we are."

"I was so worried you were going to tell me that you wanted to stop seeing me. That's why I didn't want to talk. You were so mad."

"I was, but I don't think I am anymore."

"I'm so happy to hear that. Does this mean that you still want to date? I guess what I am asking is, do you want to be my girl?"

"Your girl?"

"I know it sounds corny. But I thought 'be my girlfriend' would be even cornier."

"You're right, that would have been cornier."

Bling. I turn my head and look at my computer. It is the sound of people joining a meeting. Crap. It's time for my monthly with Carl.

"Shit! I have a meeting with Carl right now."

"Okay. I will let myself out. But don't think I forgot about the question I asked. You still need to answer it."

"I know," I quickly say before leaping over to my computer and hitting the join button. I don't even hear him leave.

How the heck am I supposed to concentrate on my monthly meeting with Carl? First, Nick asks me out, then I just hang up on him when McGruff shows up here and asks me if I still want to be with him. What the crap is even happening?

"Hi, Gemma," Carl says.

Oh, great. It's starting. Time to talk to the disembodied voice of my boss.

"Hi, Carl."

"I haven't had a one-on-one with you since we were in the office. How have these last few weeks been for you?"

"Good. There was an adjustment period. But everything has been going really well."

"I am glad to hear it. You're back in the daily meeting with us. I've been thinking, and I don't foresee you having to go to the meeting much after the requirements for P3 are set in stone."

Say what? Am I dreaming? This is definitely a dream, right? I mean, I *am* in bed. This can't be real.

"Do you think you need to be there?" he asks.

"No," I say immediately. "I don't have much to do with the project once the requirements are done."

Way to play it cool, Gemma.

"I agree. And I don't foresee you having to test P3, either. Fred and Bill should be able to cover it sufficiently."

Hallelujah! Another prayer answered. Should I dare broach the subject of continuing to work from home?

"That is great," I say.

"Yes, we have a bunch of projects in the pipeline after P3 go-live that I need you to focus your attention on."

"Sounds good to me."

That's right. Keep cool. Don't want to overplay your hand, here. Don't want him to take it back.

"Any questions?"

"When do you think we will be back in the office?"

"I think within the week we should be ready to get back in there. A few days at the most."

My heart sinks. No. I am not ready to give this up. Working from home is the best thing that has ever happened to me.

Play it cool, Gemma. Play it cool.

"I…" I start.

Yes, Gemma. Do it. You have to do it. It won't happen if you don't ask. This is your best shot. Worst that happens is that he says no. Then you move on with your life like you always do.

"I was wondering," I continue, "what the company policy is for working from home on a regular basis?"

"That's something that would interest you?"

"Yes."

Should I say something else? Add an anecdote, perhaps? A scale of how much I love it? Improv a song about it?

Shush. Play it cool.

"I have to say, your work has not suffered at all since we've been home. You still operate at a high level. We've all proven that we can do virtual meetings. I'll tell you what, I will talk to Bob about it. I imagine it will not be a full-time thing, but maybe a day or two a week at home. Would that work?"

Yes! Yes! Yes!

My heart nearly jumps out of my chest. For the first time in a long time, a sense of hope washes over me. I can see a tiny light at the end of the tunnel.

"Yes. That would work. Thank you very much, Carl."

"You're one of my best workers. We want to keep you happy, if we can."

Oh, my God. Did he say I'm one of the best? Am I his favorite? I'm his favorite, right?

"Is there anything else you want to talk about?" he asks. "I pretty much know what you're working on."

"Nope. That's it for today."

"All right. Let me know if you need anything. I will give you fifteen minutes back, and I will talk to you later."

"Okay, will do. Bye."

His name disappears from the screen, and I hit the leave meeting button. Oh, my God. Did that just happen? What a weird day today is.

I want to tell someone! I want to tell everyone! Should I run down the hall and tell Walter? Should I call Liz? McGruff? Brittany? Nick?

Hold your horses. You don't even know if it's happening yet. Bob could say no.

He could. And you know what? I can quit.

Whoa. What are you talking about?

I've been so unhappy for a while now, and these last couple of weeks have given me a glimpse of a life and a job that I don't have to stress over, that I can actually do without hating myself on a regular basis. I have hope that I can find this peace and comfort again, even if it happens to be at another company.

Okay. Calm down. Why don't you wait to see what Bob says first? Finding and starting another job is scary.

Yes. It is, so I will wait to see what Bob says. But I am not ready to give up this feeling yet, this feeling of contentment with my job and how I react and deal with it.

Good. Now, who are you going to call?

I know who, but I have to give him an answer first. And I guess if he's on the top of my list to call, then my answer is going to be yes.

I pick up my phone and scroll down until I see his number. I hit the video chat button and watch my nervous face wait for an answer.

What if he doesn't answer? I should hang up.

No. Just see if he answers.

And he does. His face appears. He looks apprehensive.

"Hey," he says.

"I hope I'm not interrupting anything. I didn't mean to call out of nowhere. I just got some encouraging news from Carl, and I wanted to share."

I can see his whole body relax and his face soften. "Well, do tell."

"Okay, so you know how I adore working from home? I asked Carl about still doing it going forward, after the building is reopened, and he said he'd talk to Bob about it. But he said it might only be a day or two, so I don't want to get excited."

"That's awesome, Gemma! And I think you are excited already, which is nice to see. I think it will work out. I know it."

"I hope so. But my hopes are already up, so I hope I don't get crushed."

His eyes dart to the side and then back at me. I guess his hopes are up, too.

"Yeah, and I wanted to answer your question from earlier."

He takes a deep breath and holds it.

"Yes, I do."

His lips curve into a smile, and his eyes sparkle.

Why do his eyes always sparkle at me like that?

CHAPTER SIXTEEN

My eyes slowly roll open, and I scan my studio apartment.

What is that noise? It's a beeping. What could be beeping?

That's your alarm, Gemma.

What? My alarm? No, that's just for show. It never wakes me up. I always wake up before it, if not hours before it. Always.

I stretch my arm over and switch off the beeping.

Wow. I slept to my alarm. I can't remember the last time that happened. I must have been a kid.

Rolling onto my back, I stretch my arms up over my head. My eyes pop open wide.

I have to go back to the office today. I have to physically go back to the office. I have to get dressed in normal clothes and interact with other humans in person. Can I do that anymore? No, I definitely cannot.

Just breathe. You are fine.

I close my eyes and slowly inhale and then slowly exhale.

My eyes pop open again. My heart isn't racing. What is up with that? Why isn't my heart racing? Where is my constant frenemy, my anxiety?

Why are you freaking out about not freaking out? This is a good thing. Please don't ruin this.

It's just weird not having anxiety. It is the one constant in my life.

Stop this! You are now having anxiety about not having anxiety. Please stop this madness.

Fine. I pull on my skirt and blouse, slip on my heels, and look in the mirror. I guess this will do. It's no leggings and T-shirt, but I don't think the HR department would really like that.

Grabbing my purse, I head down the elevator and out of the building. I brace for impact as I open the door to the outside.

Huh. It's not scorching hot outside today. Not yet anyway. And it is Friday. So today might not be so bad after all. You can do this.

As I walk down the street, Sally's comes in to view. And there he is, my dazzling guy, standing nonchalantly next to Sally's holding two cups. His eyes light up when he sees me.

"Good morning," he says and lightly kisses me.

"Morning."

"I got a coffee and a tea. I didn't know what you wanted. Whichever you don't want, I will drink."

"I'll take the tea. Thank you."

"Tea?"

"Yeah. Back to the office. I have to go back to normal and try to limit my caffeine intake."

He hands me the cup, takes my hand with the now empty hand, and kisses me again.

"You're happy today," I say.

"What's not to be happy about?"

"Returning to the office?"

"Yeah, but I get to see you, though. I missed this."

"Seeing you is the only thing I missed about the office."

He stops walking and kisses me again.

"You're not even complaining about the heat this morning," he says.

"It's not actually that bad."

"Wow."

"Yeah, the office is enough to complain about."

He opens the door to the lobby and lets me walk in first. There are people here. Why am I no longer used to being around people? How quickly we learn new habits.

I sigh as we get crammed into the back of the elevator, now packed with bodies. I did not miss this.

Just breathe.

Slowly the people leave floor by floor, and the elevator doors shut and leave the two of us alone.

"What are you thinking about?" he asks.

"Coffee."

"I told you that you could have it."

"I know. But not drinking it is for the best. I just miss it already."

He kisses me once more as the doors open on floor twenty. Stepping out, he turns to smile as the doors close on his beautiful face.

Thankfully, Nick is not at his desk when I walk by. Unlocking my computer, I pull up my email. There is a meeting invite from Carl just called, "Quick Meeting."

If there were ever a meeting to get fired in, this is it.

He's not going to fire you. He just told you that you're one of his best employees.

He could have changed his mind. Would it be that bad if he did?

I accept the meeting and notice that another has just come in, only, it's not an invite, it's a cancellation. Carl has officially taken me off of the daily meeting. It's officially wiped from my calendar.

I switch over to calendar view just to make sure. Yep. It's gone. Every day, it's gone. What a sweet feeling this is.

Kind of anticlimactic. You just get a cancellation via email? After years of work and meetings, this is how it ends?

Who cares! It's over!

Shouldn't there be some sort of fanfare?

Like what? A ticker tape parade down the aisle?

You spent so long working and obsessing about this meeting. Don't you think there should be something?

I am taking this win and moving on.

Moving on? Since when do you not obsess about everything?

Today, I guess.

I hear rustling next to me. Nick is settling in.

Crap. Why did I think that he would just not show up, and I'd never have to face him again? Why did I think that somehow it would be fine seeing him again, like I didn't refuse to go out with him?

It will be fine. You are both adults. He knew going into this whole situation that you were dating someone. It is not your fault.

Then why do I feel like it is?

Carl brushes past me, extends his arm in my direction in a wave, and then heads down the aisle towards the conference room for the daily meeting.

I guess that is the most fanfare I am going to get. There is my ticker tape parade.

I catch a glimpse of Brittany scurrying into the room as Nick walks by my desk and awkwardly smiles, but he doesn't look directly at me.

I am assuming that smile is for me? Why is no one looking directly at me today? Do I look like a hideous monster? Why didn't McGruff tell me? I am not used to being out of my apartment, out with people all around. I don't know how to act.

You never knew how to act.

Harsh. But fair.

He is just avoiding you because you completely crushed his heart. That is all.

No, I didn't. Did I? Everything will go back to normal, right?

Doubt it.

My heartbeat quickens. Ah, there is my steadfast companion. I knew it couldn't be gone.

Why are you relieved that your anxiety is back? You should be relieved that it is gone.

I sigh and open the quick meeting that Carl invited me to. It is immediately after the daily meeting and in the same room. Great. I get to have another awkward encounter with Nick. Maybe he will just ignore me this time.

Gem of Uncertainty

I stroll down to stand in front of the conference room. It is a strange sensation to now be the legs standing outside, waiting for the meeting to end, but it never does. I am not in there praying for those legs to bust in and demand that the meeting end. And I am certainly not going to do that. Sorry, Brittany.

Should I just go back to my desk and wait? I can see when people leave. I should have just done that to begin with. Now, I am stupidly standing here waiting for the never-ending meeting to end.

Just wait it out. Do you really want to be at your desk? Your work is there. If Carl is truly firing you, then why spend your last few minutes actually working?

He is not firing me. Everything will be fine.

Then why did he cancel your daily meeting? Maybe he is just preparing.

Stop it! Everything is fine. I am fine.

Feet begin to stir in the conference room. The meeting is coming to a close. Bill is the first to leave. Then Nick, who looks quizzically at me as he walks by. I guess that is better than earlier. Brittany is last.

"Where were you?" she asks.

"I don't have to go anymore. I have a meeting with Carl now. I will talk to you after."

She nods as I enter the conference room, close the door, and sit across from Carl.

"So," he says, "I took you off of the daily meeting."

I definitely saw that. "Yes."

"You did a great job on Bookroll, Gemma. I am glad that you are on our team."

This is it. He is firing you.

"Thank you."

"That being said. You are a vital part of our team, Gemma. I talked to Bob about what we talked about in our last meeting."

And he told you to fire me because of it?

"And he has agreed to allow you to work from home on Monday and Friday on a trial basis."

Is he serious? He seems serious. Can this just be an elaborate joke?

"Really?"

"Yes, really, Gemma. These last few weeks have shown that we, as a company, can continue to do business and be productive while working from home. Some jobs are more suited to working from home than others, and while you will still be needed in meetings, we feel that you can participate virtually, and your work will not suffer."

Hallelujah! This is not a drill. This is happening.

A smile spreads across my face.

"Thank you so much."

"You are very welcome. Obviously, today is Friday, and even though you are already here, and I didn't run this by Bob, but you can work from home for the rest of the day today. I know you live close by, so you won't miss much work on the way home."

Is he kidding? Is this really happening? Is this the same Carl that has been my boss for years?

"Thank you, Carl. This really means a lot to me."

"You deserve it, Gemma. As I told you before, you are one of my best employees. I'd like to keep you happy, if I can."

Holy shit. Why didn't I do this earlier?

You weren't ready. But you are now.

"Okay, well that was it on my end," Carl says. "Is there anything you'd like to talk about?"

"No. I just want to thank you, again."

"It is my pleasure," he says as he gets up and leaves the room.

Should I pinch myself? Should I run home and get back into my leggings? Should I shout thanks to the heavens?

I should go tell Brittany.

Getting up, I speed walk down the aisle before skidding to a stop when I round the corner and see Nick standing in front of Brittany's desk.

I should come back later.

No, be a big girl and go over. He can't make a scene in the middle of work.

But I don't make the decision. They both turn to look at me, standing in the middle of the aisle and staring back at them.

All right. Pull up your big girl pants, and go over.

And I do. Brittany smiles and waves and Nick just blankly stares at me. He makes a motion to leave, but Brittany stops him.

"Hey!" Brittany says as I get close.

I stand a few feet away from Nick, near the opening of Brittany's cube.

"Where were you today," she asks.

"Carl cancelled my meeting series. I don't have to go anymore."

"Lucky!" she shouts. "You must be so happy."

"I am," I say, devoid of any emotion.

"You don't seem like it," she responds.

"I'll go," Nick says.

"No, don't go," Brittany says. "We used to be a pack. I want us to be, again."

"Brittany…" I say.

"I would like to be a pack again, too," Nick says quietly.

"You do?" I ask.

"Of course. You are my work wives. My work harem, if you will."

"No," Brittany says, "I will not let you call us that. That is not what we are."

"Yeah, I knew the second that came out of my mouth that it wouldn't go over well," Nick says.

"Lunch today, then?" Brittany asks.

"I'm in," Nick responds.

They both look at me.

"Well, that's what I came over to tell you. Carl told me that I can work from home every Monday and Friday, and he is letting me work from home for the rest of the day, today."

"That's amazing!" Brittany says. "You must be so excited."

"I am."

"That is awesome, Gemma," Nick says. "I am really happy for you. However, that is no excuse to not come to lunch with us. We know how close you live, and it is not grossly hot out today."

"Yeah!" Brittany shouts. "What he said!"

"But…"

"No buts," Brittany says. "We are a pack."

"Okay, fine. I will meet you at the park for lunch."

"Yes!" Brittany shouts. "We got her."

"I will see you two there, then," Nick says and walks away.

"What did you say to him?" I ask Brittany once Nick is out of hearing range.

"Nothing."

"Yes, you did."

"Fine. I tried to smooth things over. We were such a good pack before this thing. I told him that he knew you were dating someone, so he can't be upset. He knew about Nate from the start."

"He was okay with just staying friends?"

"Yep."

"What aren't you telling me?"

"Nothing."

"Brittany…"

"You didn't want me to tell you what I told you last time about Nick liking you."

"Yes, I remember that. But you can tell me this time."

"Okay, just don't get weirded out."

"I won't."

Yes, you will. No matter what she tells you, you will get weirded out.

"Okay. He said that he'd wait it out."

"Wait it out?"

"Yeah, you and McGruff."

"Brittany!"

"I told you that you wouldn't want to know."

"I can't go to lunch now."

"Yes, you can. We are just a pack like we used to be."

"I am definitely with McGruff. There is no wavering this time."

"I know. Nick will get over it, I promise."

"Okay, well, I am going home. Let me know when lunch is. I may or may not come down."

"Yes, you will."

"Maybe."

"Yes."

We stare at each other until I turn around and walk away. I can hear her say, "Yes," once more as I turn the corner.

Sitting at my desk, I pull my phone out of my purse and text McGruff. "Are you in a meeting? Meet me at the elevator?"

I shove my phone back into my purse and lock my computer. So long desk. As I make the U around my desk and pass Nick's, I hear him say, "See you at lunch."

I turn to see him grinning, and I smile back. When I get to the elevator, I step over the slit of death, and push the lobby button as the doors close. The box only gets two flights down before it stops. The doors open on beautiful McGruff standing there with a concerned look. He gets in and the elevator doors close, again.

"Everything okay?" he asks.

"I got fired."

His eyes open wide. "What?"

"Just kidding!"

"You are the worst."

"I know."

"What is up, then?"

"Carl said I can work from home Monday and Friday, and then said I can go home and work for the rest of the day starting now."

"That is great! I am so happy for you!"

"Thanks," I say and smile up at him.

The elevator doors open to the lobby, and I turn to look at him as I walk out. He stays in the box.

"See you tonight?" I ask.

A broad smile spreads across his face.

"Of course, you're my girl, aren't you?"

"I guess I am," I say as the doors close on his sparkling eyes.

Smiling, I twirl around.

Did you just twirl?

Yes, I am a twirler now.

I hop forward and practically skip to the door.

Did you just hop?

Yes, I am a hopper now.

What is happening?

Nothing. I am just happy.

I scamper down the street to my apartment building, up the elevator, and into my apartment. Kicking off my heels, I strip off my skirt and blouse and replace them with leggings and a T-shirt. Grabbing my laptop, I turn it on, and carry it over to my bed. Getting under the covers, I put the laptop on my lap and wait for it to boot up.

I should call Walter. Maybe he will bring over some coffee.

I let my head relax against the pillow and inhale deeply. A girl could get used to this.